Giraffe of
Montana

VOLUME IV

William Bowman Piper

Little Pemberley Press
Houston, TX
2008

Little Pemberley Press
1528 Tulane Street, Suite F
Houston, TX 77008
713-862-8542

www.GiraffeofMontana.com

ISBN# 978-0-9763359-7-9

Piper, William Bowman, 1927-
    Giraffe of Montana / by William Bowman Piper.
    p. cm. — (Giraffe of Montana ; v. 4)
    SUMMARY: A giraffe living in Montana and his animal
friends share adventures and the ups and downs of daily life.
    Audience: Ages 6-13.
    ISBN 0-9763359-7-9

    1. Animals—Juvenile fiction. [1. Animals—Fiction.
    2. Friendship—Fiction. 3. Montana—Fiction.] I. Title.

    PZ10.3.P412Gir 2005   [E] QBI05-600033

Book Production Team
Consulting & Coordination — Rita Mills of The Book Connection

Cover Design & Illustration — Bill Megenhardt

The paper used in this publication meets the requirements of the American National Stan-
dard for Permanence of Paper for Printed Library Materials Z39.48-1984.

Printed in the United States of America

for Faye

Table of Contents

Arrival

The last Queen Isabel saw of Giraffe after they had said their goodbyes at the cross-tracks in Camelot on the day of the victory celebration he was limping east down the trail that led through Montana woods toward the badlands of Dakota and, beyond Dakota, to Iowa, Illinois, Indiana, Ohio, and Kentucky.

Giraffe did not limp all the way to Kentucky, however, nor even as far as

Illinois. He paused, instead, on secret orders from King Arthur, in the vast, forbidding, and desolate badlands of Dakota.

He and the king had met in private consultation several times in the weeks after the Round Table's victory over the Survivalists, and they had discussed at length a plan of Arthur's.

"I have recently achieved a reconciliation, Giraffe," the king told him confidentially, "with my British druid, Merlin, from whom I was estranged for many centuries."

"I suppose that means, my lord," said Giraffe, whom the knights were beginning to call "Arthur's Montana druid," "you will no longer need my services."

"Far from it, my friend," said the king, giving Giraffe a pat below the knee. "Aside from the fact Merlin's captor, the Lady Nyneve, has only lent him to me on parole, you are more important to me and the Lady Isabel and to all our subjects than ever before. Merlin understands power; and I have studied war. My present concerns, however, require, not these skills, Giraffe, but yours. I wish you to serve me in my old home, the Borders of Britain, where I still have some unfinished business."

"The Borders of Britain, my lord! I have hardly ever traveled outside Montana in my whole adult life—except for a brief train ride to the Florida Zoo."

"War and peace are the same the world over, Giraffe, and, to fulfill my designs in the Borders now, that is, in my own time and place, I need your talent for peace."

"How can I reach your time and place, my lord? Look at the gray hairs between these horns; look at this creaky hip; consider this bandage. It's true, now Fergus and Isabella have assumed the duties of rule in the middle of Montana, I plan to wander into Illinois, perhaps, and, if my strength and my bandage hold out, to visit Ohio and Indiana and Kentucky. But the Borders—during your own time? What whirlwind can take me there?"

"Your crippled hip, Giraffe, need carry you no further than the badlands of Dakota. Once you get there, you must pause," Arthur commanded, "and reach out, as Merlin has directed, to Trimontium, the heart of the Borders. You must reach out from the badlands, Giraffe, and grasp my British druid or, rather, submit yourself to my British druid's grasp."

"How can I reach out, my lord, with my tongue?"

"With your mind, Giraffe, with your mind. Merlin, whose power is temporarily focused in the badlands," the king assured him, "will transport you, he has promised me, to the base of Eildon North, the greatest of Trimontium's three enchanted peaks."

"Trimontium? Your ancient home? What would you have me do, my lord," Giraffe asked, "once I have—landed there?"

"When I had driven the Saxons south of the Wall," Arthur explained or began to explain, "and scattered the raiders on my western flank and earned some breathing space for Rheged, Gododdin, and Strathclyde, the Celtic kingdoms under my protection, I should have made peace with the Picts. There was time for that."

"Time to make peace with the Picts, my lord?" Giraffe exclaimed.

"The Picts are Celts, just like us, Giraffe, and they have become organized under Drust, 'who fought a hundred battles' (three against me), and under his successor, Nechton the freckled (freckled like all his countrymen). I could have sent envoys east to the Catertuns or north to Craig Phadraig; I could have sent Gawain or Lancelot, both of whom have Pictish freckles on their faces. But I missed the chance. It was partly because of the betrayal of my Pictish queen, Guinevere the freckled—about which everybody knows; but that merely poisoned an already noxious political climate. The Picts were our foes; they had raided the Roman province again-and-again; they had repelled the legions of the great Roman general, Agricola, below the White Catertuns centuries before and remained a thorn in our side ever since—in our *Roman* side. That's what we said; and no doubt what they said too. So we both cultivated hostility. What a waste, Giraffe, what a mistake."

"But I was told in school," Giraffe said, "the Picts were naked barbaric savages, whose warty bodies were painted all over, warriors full of hideous valor, who shrieked and charged without fear or order—just a crazy, drunken rout."

"The Picts are Celts, Giraffe, as I told you, Celts, just like the two of us. It was the Romans who painted them. Neither Agricola nor Antonine nor Severus could conquer the Picts, so they smeared them with lies. But no matter what those Romans said, I should have befriended them. The Picts are wonderful people, handsome (despite their freckles), brave, superstitious, and very artistic. Did you ever see their stone carvings?"

"No, my lord, I haven't," Giraffe admitted.

"Of course not. But take my word for it, they are beautiful works. The stone slab at Aberlemno in southern Pictland, which was carved a couple of centuries after my time to depict one of their triumphs over the Saxons, is a masterpiece. The sculpted interlace on the front side of it, the figures of spearmen and mounted troops and the pulse of battle on the reverse. I wish I could have lived to see it. The Picts are magnificent people. They are our people, moreover, and I should have tried to befriend them.

"I'm not just remembering the help they might have given me when Mordred stole my queen nor when, at the calamitous battle of Camlann, feisty elements among my own folks turned their swords against me. No, I'm thinking about the lost benefits and the squandered opportunities for cooperation there might have been between our two nations. If Nechton and I had reached a firm understanding, our people on both sides of the Forth—Celts all—might have enjoyed the chance provided by a peaceful border to pursue their individual desires instead of ceaselessly whetting themselves for war."

"I understand your feelings, my lord," said Giraffe. "I love peace; I have always advocated individual exertion and individual fulfillment—life, liberty and the pursuit of happiness, as a long-forgotten American once described it. But I am at a loss, nevertheless, to understand my mission in Pictland. I can't see what you would have me do when I have re-joined you and Isabel and the others in your old home."

"I want a second chance, Giraffe," the king explained looking way up into the eyes of his friend and counsellor.

"A second chance, my lord? A second chance to establish peace between yourself and the ancient Picts?"

"Exactly. As you traverse Eildon North with Merlin, Giraffe, you will alter, not only your elevation on earth, but also your relation to history: the higher you climb around that magic mound, the further you will recede in time. One circuit will bring you face-to-face with Thomas the Rhymer, the famous laureate of Trimontium; on the second, you will encounter Aneirin, the grieving bard of the ill-fated Gododdin; and at the right point of the third circuit, as you climb higher-and-higher—not to the top, Giraffe, or you will find yourselves in the stone age, but at the right point—Merlin will recognize and he will show you my own time and place."

"Your own time and place in history, my lord?"

"Yes, Giraffe, the British Borders during the fifth cenutury, my own time and place. And there you two, you and Merlin, with the assistance of local folk and itinerant dragons, must build the Lady Isabel, my knights, and me a great hall of wood and stone—no plastics, Giraffe. Use Scottish oak for the pillars and the beams and good Caledonian pine for the floor and the walls. Then you must go west into Ettrick Forest and find beavers to work the withes of willow and hazel and weave the roof."

"Beavers, my lord? Can beavers in the Borders perform that task?"

"Naturally, Giraffe. Do you think British beavers are inferior to these in Montana?"

14

"No, I imagine beavers have the same skills the world over. But what comes next, my lord, after the hall has been built and roofed?"

"Our furniture, of course, and it must be fashioned, not by raccoons (there are no raccoons in the Borders), but by holy shakers from the abbeys of Kelso and Melrose and Lindisfarne—wonderful artists, whom you and Merlin will awaken to the task. This furniture—and especially the Round Table—must be crafted of mahogany, as you might have guessed, solid mahogany. Merlin has probably never heard of this exotic lumber, Giraffe, but you will help him to discover and transport it. We must take all necessary measures to assure the comfort and happiness of my Lady Isabel. You can hardly imagine, Giraffe, how ardently I admire and love her, but you surely know I can not be happy without her."

"I have come to understand the love you share with her, my lord," Giraffe said. "But what next after we have furnished your hall?"

"Then," said the king, "you will order the smiths at Traprain Law to cast me a great bronze Gundestrup bowl, a proper bowl," he said with anticipatory relish, "for cheese and bananas."

"I will try, my lord."

"With the assistance of Merlin and the local craftsmen, Giraffe, you will succeed.

"Then, once our new hall is built, roofed, and furnished and when the Round Table is set, you and Merlin will descend upon Dakota, swooping through the dark of

Samain Eve, to carry us—knights and dragons and all—back to our rightful spot."

"I realize, my lord," Giraffe said, swinging his tongue from side-to-side, "you and your knights have come to call me a druid, a wizard, but I'm afraid this trick is beyond my power—or the power of anyone."

"Of any *one,* perhaps," Arthur conceded, "but with Merlin there will be two, two great wizards. And if you can enlist Thomas the Rhymer, about whose imaginative grasp of time you should remind Merlin, there will be three, three mighty magicians, to gather my knights and my queen and me all together on the three magical slopes of Trimontium."

So here was Giraffe waiting in the badlands for Merlin, that disciple of the dark. It was the right place. "Was it Sheriff Cody," Giraffe asked himself, "who told me the badlands looked like Hades after the fires were put out?"

Low buttes and meager bluffs surrounded him. Their naked layers of rock, layers that proclaimed a million years of exposure, presented a wild range of colors, firey reds and oranges and purples and golds among the dominant seams of gray, hot colors that changed as the unblinking sun drove across the sky. Stuck in among these gaudy desolate acres of peaks and shelves and ridges were countless little gorges, failed canyons, on the seared slopes of which a mean foliage—brown sage, prickly bracken, black moss, and other parched grasses—clung for life and strained for nourishment. In a crevice here-and-there on the craggy sides of these gorges flared warped and weathered junipers; and down in the gullies between them, where hot water gathered or through which it flowed, stood a few stunted cottonwoods.

The badland rocks had as many shapes as colors—cones, arches, rims, needles, bowls, spurs, obelisks—shapes that seemed, as hard as the rocks were, to change as the colors changed. Once Giraffe thought he saw Ella the elephant: "That was Ella's silhouette alright." But in a moment it became Zack the zebra with rainbow stripes running the wrong way; then, as the rays of the sun slid on, it turned into a squat, dappled arch. "Nobody could mistake that formation, let me tell you," Giraffe said to himself, "for Hal the hippo."

Running through these tortured seams of rock, as he came gradually to see, were fuses of black, black coal, so, as he told himself, "At any moment the fires of Hades might be kindled again."

Just as he said that, he felt a tiny chill between his ears and his horns, a cold, damp breeze astir in the withering, stagnant atmosphere. "Strange," he said, "a minute ago the air seemed to be as still as the air in an oven." Then as he watched, a tiny twister, a whirl of sparkling rainbow dust, appeared under Ella's petrified trunk.

It advanced toward Giraffe, who stood rooted in place, and as it advanced it grew. Seeming to spin faster-and-faster, it approached Arthur's druid as he gazed and wondered. At last it completely encircled him, hoofs, horns and all, a glittering spiral of dust, and then—

And then he was gone from the badlands.

"Welcome, my friend," said a slender man with a long, black beard and tight green britches, addressing Giraffe, who was stamping his hooves, stretching his neck and trying to get his bearings. "Welcome," he said again as he tucked his beard into his belt: "welcome to the Borders and the land of Gododdin."

After a pause, during which he adjusted his pointed green hat and raised his matching green eyes, he continued, "I'd know you anywhere, naturally—or supernaturally: I am a wizard, after all. You are Giraffe, King Arthur's Montana druid. Welcome to my world, Giraffe, and to the beleagured realm of the Celts. I hope your trip was easy."

"Very easy indeed," Giraffe replied, looking closely at his new colleague. "Merlin, I presume."

"Dr. Merlin, if you please," said the host, tipping his hat to his enormous guest, and he produced a black leather satchel bulging, apparently, with magical devices.

"Dr. Merlin, if you will pardon me," said the courteous foreigner and bent his head way down in apology. "I wonder, Dr. Merlin, if you might assure me of my whereabouts. This is surely not Montana nor Dakota either. We are standing together on the peak of a beautiful green hill I see, but is it a peak of Trimontium? That is the destination to which King Arthur has commanded me."

"No, Giraffe," replied Arthur's British druid, "I have brought you to The Cheviot. From here, if you turn to the northwest, you will see Trimontium standing beside the Tweed. The land stretching from here to there and on beyond to the Moorfoot Hills and the land stretching northeastward beyond the Lammermuirs and the land reaching due east to the sea is Arthur's domain. If you follow the Teviot River lying just below us, as it runs east and north to join the Tweed, you will catch a glimpse of Arthur's old fort, Roxborough (as it came to be called) where the two streams meet. This seemed to me to be the right vantage for you to introduce yourself to your new home."

"Thank you," said Arthur's Montana druid to Arthur's British druid as he turned to survey the expanding scene. "The woods, as far as my eyes can see, are fresh and full; the hills provide green pasturage to their tops; the plains are apparently fertile; and the streams, as I can tell even from this distance, flow clear and clean. It will be delightful to live in such a time and place."

"We have moors here, as you will discover, Giraffe," said Dr. Merlin, giving his tartan cloak a twitch, "desolate reaches of rock and bogs, but no badlands—the more's the pity: I felt right at home there."

"I am very grateful to you for this introduction," said Giraffe, who was beginning to recover from being spun half way around the world, "but would not your lord and mine wish us to make our way to Trimontium and set ourselves about his business?"

"Quite right," said Dr. Merlin with a smile. "We'd better head on over to Eildon North and begin to build that hall of Arthur's."

"But how?" asked Giraffe, looking down the steep slope of The Cheviot, to the edge of which Dr. Merlin had transported him. "I'm not sure I can make it down from here with this crazy hip of mine. We giraffes move more easily on level ground."

"Then I fancy we'll have to fly," the doctor said with a reassuring firmness. "It's not far."

"I'm afraid," said Giraffe, who was afraid, "it's a lot farther than I can fly."

"Just follow me," said Dr. Merlin, "I know the way."

"The way to fly?" asked Giraffe.

"The way to Trimontium," answered the British druid. And as he spoke, he fastened the four corners of his cloak to gold bands on his wrists and ankles, checked his beard, and pulled his hat down over his ears. The cloak was beautifully woven and, as the doctor extended his arms in the sunlight, he resembled a butterfly.

"A many-colored butterfly," Giraffe said to himself.

But then, when Dr. Merlin turned toward his guest and smiled, showing buck teeth through his heavy black beard, Giraffe corrected himself: "Not a butterfly," he murmured, "but a bat, a green-eyed bat with iridescent wings."

When Dr. Merlin flapped his arms and took off, he

did fly with the erratic darts and dashes of a bat. "Come on," he cried over his shoulder, "follow me!"

Before Giraffe could shout after him to ask him how, he felt strange swellings in both his shoulders; and then, before he was able to check them, buds began thrusting up into the sunlight and unfurled as they grew. "I'm sprouting wings, dragon's wings, Charlton's wings," he gasped. And before he realized the danger, a stiff breeze off The Cheviot caught in these magical acquisitions and bore him into the sky.

"Follow me," cried the doctor as he darted back toward Giraffe and away: "follow me."

Giraffe wanted to reply that he couldn't follow him. "I don't know how these things work," he tried to shout. But before he could, he found he did know how; and giving a thunderous beat to Charlton's wings, he soared off after his flickering friend.

As he glided along, becoming increasingly comfortable on his wings, Giraffe watched the doctor flap and flutter. "He surely works hard to keep aloft," Giraffe said to himself.

Dr. Merlin soon reached a good altitude above the old Roman road—

"Dere Street," Giraffe murmured and wondered where he'd learned that—

And he followed it for a mile or two to Eildon North. Then, with a wild flutter, he swung left and, flapping his cloak vigorously to keep his balance, landed at the hill's wooded base.

Giraffe, soaring behind him, lowered his left wing

and, giving one final beat, came in smoothly for a four hoof landing.

"Well, Giraffe," said Dr. Merlin as he struggled to get his breath, "how did you like your flight?"

"Thank you, doctor," Giraffe answered with a smile, "much better than my trip across the Atlantic."

"If I had stuck you with wings in the badlands, my friend," replied King Arthur's British druid while he unfastened his cloak from his wrists and ankles, smoothed his beard, and readjusted his hat, "you'd still be flying somewhat west of Greenland, I figure, and that's if you caught favorable winds."

"That may be, Dr. Merlin," said Giraffe, "but I wouldn't have gotten so dizzy and disoriented."

"Maybe not," the doctor acknowledged, "but Arthur doesn't have time to provide you first-class passage everyplace. By the way, you can call me Merlin now—since we've flown together."

"What next, then, Merlin?"

"This way," said the druid, "round and round, up and up, until we reach Arthur's time and place."

And Giraffe, who realized his wings had vanished without a trace, followed, somewhat sad to find how hard it was to walk once again, especially on his bad leg.

After they had climbed for an hour or so single file on a path that would have been too faint for Giraffe to see, they circled a boulder and met—

"Thomas," Merlin exclaimed, "Thomas the Rhymer. How's tricks, Thomas? Any new time warps?"

"No, Merlin, I'm just waiting and wondering. My love, Gruoch the faye, told me five-hundred years ago to the day that she'd be back, so here I stay."

"She's not worth your patience, Thomas," said Merlin. "She's pretty enough by day no doubt, but at night, they tell me, she's a hag, a loathly hag; and it's the night that matters, that is, in matters of love."

"You may talk, Merlin—with a girl friend like the constant Nyneve—but I'm Gruoch's slave both day and night. Night and day Gru reigns serene; under sunshine or moonlight no matter, Gru is my queen."

"Gruoch," Merlin explained to Giraffe, who had been huffing and puffing behind him and was just catching up, "Gruoch," he whispered, " means witch or fairy to us."

"To you, Merlin, and people like you," Thomas said, looking at Giraffe with severity, "that's true." And turning from them, he chanted in a thin melancholy voice, "Flying for laughs with a herd of giraffes is my notion of nothing to do; but I get a kick out of Gru. Actually," he said, lowering his voice and wiping his eyes with the tail of his faded red jerkin, "I haven't got a kick out of anything for five-hundred years now.

"You are Giraffe, aren't you?" he asked, turning with a little smile toward Arthur's Montana druid.

"Yes," said Giraffe, "I'm flattered to think you would recognize me, Thomas. But do you believe Gruoch has really deserted you?"

23

"Yes," said the Rhymer with a sigh, "it was just one of those things, just one of those Cheviot springs, a flight into space on removable wings; it was just one of those things."

"She may reappear one of these days," said Giraffe sympathetically.

"No," said the Rhymer, "it was just one gaudy night—

("A seven-year night, or so I've heard," said Merlin to Giraffe)—

"Just one meager marvellous flight, a visit to stars, Orion and Mars, it was just one gaudy night."

"At any rate," said Merlin matter-of-factly, "before Gruoch dumped you, she endowed you with some power over time, time future and time past—or so the story goes. And right now, Thomas, Giraffe and I need all the power you've got, don't we, Giraffe?"

"Yes," Arthur's other druid agreed, "a little of your elastic command of time would help us provide our lord Arthur a second chance."

"A second chance to do what? to win back Guinevere?" said the sentimental Rhymer.

"No," Giraffe replied, "a second chance to make peace with the Picts."

"Oh, politics," said the Rhymer.

"Yes, old boy," Merlin said. "You know how kings are. Well, what do you say?"

"If Arthur's the man," the Rhymer answered, "I'll do what I can.

"I suppose," he said with a sigh, "If Gru should ever need a rhyme, she can find me any time."

Then turning away from Merlin and Giraffe, he consoled himself. "If I'd thought of it, at the start of it, when we started fooling around, I'd have seen, it's true, that my choice of Gru was altogether unsound." And with that he stood up, gave a last look at the rock he'd been sitting on for five-hundred years, and fell in behind Merlin and Giraffe.

The three of them trudged on around Eildon North for a while, walking in deep shade, which was punctuated by the moaning of doves. That seemed, Giraffe noticed, perfectly to suit the Rhymer's mood.

Then as they stumbled around the trunk of a huge oak, they came upon—

Aneirin, as Arthur had predicted. He was very shabby: his plaid coat was frayed, and there were gaping holes in the knees of his hose. But the harp, which he cradled on his lap, was quite fine, inlaid with ivory snakes and flowers and vines. He was huddled alone on a big stump, strumming and weeping.

"They're all dead," he wailed, "only I am left to tell the story." And he twanged the strings of his harp.

"Would you like to hear it?" he asked hopefully as the three masters of magic gathered around him.

"I am very willing to recite," he said after blowing his nose on a tattered saddle cloth that normally served him as a cushion or a blanket; and he gazed with eager anticipation at each of them in turn. "My tale is very sad," he promised, "but very heroic, and quite long."

Thomas was about to admit a sad tale would give him a lot of pleasure, but before he could speak, Merlin interrupted. "Thank you, Aneirin," he said as he brushed past the grieving bard, "we'll catch you on the way down;" and he hurried on.

"We'd have been there an age listening to that dreary stuff," he explained under his breath as they left Aneirin, who was tuning his harp, "and we've got things to do."

As they turned around a boulder they could hear the bard, still twanging his strings and lamenting, "Only I am left to hear the story."

After they hiked on for a spell, they reached a fork in the path.

"Which way, Thomas?" Merlin asked, "you know these hills."

"Indeed I do," the Rhymer admitted, "my teacher was Gru."

"Well then," said Merlin impatiently, "which way? Giraffe and I don't have five-hundred years. We're on a schedule."

"We should take the left fork," Thomas advised.

"The right one ends at the age of stone where lanterns gawk from teetering poles and demons prod distracted souls with sizzling flesh on splintered bone, where cattle are lashed by drunken seers down bristling rows of fire and spears. It's very interesting up there, but very windy."

"Some other time," said Merlin; "right now we had better get along to Arthur's time and place. We've got a lot to do there, haven't we, Giraffe? And it has to be done by Samain."

They followed the left fork of the path, all of them puffing a little now, with Thomas in front and Giraffe limping along behind Merlin.

For a while Arthur's Montana druid heard nothing beyond the noises of the hill and the woods—rustling leaves, trickling water, the flitting of finches, and the occasional moaning of doves—except for Thomas, who was chanting mournfully under his breath, "Goodbye, Gru, my old dear, here's hoping you come back some year."

But between the pauses in Thomas's lament, Giraffe began to detect something new, something that grew louder as the little company advanced, not Gru's overdue return, but the sound of construction. More and more clearly as they mounted Eildon North toward Arthur's time and place, Giraffe heard the cries of voices raised in a single, concerted effort and, interspersed among these cries, the rip of the saw, the beat of hammers, and the groan of timber being forced into place.

"Merlin," he said in great surprise, "you have already made a start on Arthur's hall."

"More than a start!" he exclaimed as the little party emerged from the trees and entered what was evidently a very busy building site.

The oaken pillars of a new basilica were, in fact,

completely erected and its pine frame almost completely attached. A crew of raccoons—five-or-six of them—were hammering the last timbers to the apse at the east end of the structure. Another crew, whose members constantly called for direction on a big graying raccoon named "Sammy," were dressing pine boards for the floor, carrying them inside, and with the help of a giant bull—"That fellow is almost as big as Ella," Giraffe muttered—muscling them into place.

"Arthur told me there were not any raccoons in the Borders," Giraffe said to Merlin. "Have these immigrated since he moved to Montana?"

"No," Merlin said with a laugh. "The boss has just forgotten; after all, Giraffe, fifteen-hundred years have passed since he lived here. And the truth is, there weren't any raccoons living on the isle of Avalon, where he convalesced after his last fight, the one at Camlann."

"He also told me," Giraffe said uncertainly, "beavers would be working here. Are there any beavers left in the Borders?"

"Yes," Merlin assured him, "we have a thriving population of beavers, but those in our crew are busy just now floating mahogany down the Tweed to Trimontium. Unfortunately, we don't have any heroic Montana crocodiles to handle that job."

"Mahogany, Merlin?" Giraffe cried. "I see that Arthur underestimated his British druid."

"Not really, Giraffe, Arthur sent a couple of families of dragons over with you, the Fruits and Vegetables, to help thatch the roof of his hall; and they brought the information about mahogany. The beavers, who unloaded several cords of that lumber at Lanark, have carted them over to the Tweed west of Peebles and launched them down the river. They should unload this fancy stuff in Melrose at the foot of Eildon North in the next day or two—in plenty of time for them to weave the thatch."

"How can dragons help thatch the roof?" Giraffe asked.

"The same way the reindeer helped at Friendship Hall," Merlin explained, "by steadying the beavers up there. I had thought to employ you for this, Giraffe, allowing the beavers to climb up your neck onto the roof and trusting you to catch any who fell with that handy tongue of yours. Arthur's new basilica is not as lofty as Friendship Hall. But this will be better.

"The dragons have been practising all week, holding their wings in check, gripping the thatch and twine so as not to tear them, and, of course, governing their breath; and each one has already chosen his own beaver. All you and I have to do now is watch."

"What job does that leave for me?" asked Giraffe, who was beginning to feel left out of this great enterprise.

"Let's see," said Merlin. And as he pulled his beard carefully out of his trousers, smoothed it down, and tucked it back in, he murmured thoughtfully, "I'll find something for you to do.

"Actually," he said after a pause, "Amos will need your help on the doors and windows. Holding the beams in place while the raccoons nail them fast will take both of you. Do you think you can work smoothly with Amos? I hope so."

"Amos?" Giraffe asked, "who's Amos?"

"That's Amos, Amos the aurochs," Merlin informed Giraffe: "the great bull of a fellow who's helping to lay our pine flooring.

"He's extinct," Merlin explained further, "and that makes him moody sometimes, but he's a wonderful worker. Look at the shoulder on him, Giraffe, and the span of those horns. Is he as big as Ella the elephant?"

"No, not quite," said Giraffe: "but I expect he's stronger. Does he have his horns under control—they look awfully sharp? And what about his temper?"

"Don't worry, my friend," Merlin assured Giraffe: "he's gentle as a lizard. I believe you two big fellows will be friends in no time.

"That's his companion, Elsie," Merlin said, pointing to a contented cow, the same size as those in Montana, who was chewing the cud nearby in the shade of a great chestnut tree. "She gives Amos something to live for, as he tells us sometimes when he hits one of his slumps."

"They make a beautiful couple," said Thomas with a sigh. "She's so petite and he's so strong: such a match can never go wrong."

"Without Amos," Merlin explained, "we'd never have been able to raise those oaken pillars. You'll see for yourself, Giraffe, how indispensable he is when you help him attach the doors and windows. Let me introduce you.

"Amos," he shouted, "drop that timber and come

over here for a minute? Here's some one I want you to meet."

The aurochs placed the load he had been carrying up into the hall very carefully on the ground and, with a graceful swing of his horns, turned and approached the three magicians.

"He's a fine creature," Giraffe said to himself, "although I must remember to be wary of his horns."

"Amos, this is Giraffe," said Arthur's British druid. "And this is Thomas the Rhymer. Giraffe has come over to the Borders from Montana to help you with the doors and windows. I hope you and he can work smoothly together. Go easy on him at first, he's just beginning to get his hooves on the ground."

"How do you do?" said Amos ceremoniously. "It is a pleasure for me to meet another fellow with horns—those are horns, aren't they?"

"Yes," said Giraffe, "but, as you can see, they don't amount to much—nothing like those sharp staffs of yours."

"Yes," said Amos, "they help me carry out the work Merlin has assigned me. Of course, they snag on branches and gorse sometimes when Elsie, my wife, and I trudge through the woods—and that's a nuisance."

"I was very impressed with the way you used them to move those big planks of pine. However, I'm going to have to be careful around them, no doubt, if you and I are going to work together."

"Do you find me dangerous, then?" asked Amos as he lowered his head and started to paw the ground between himself and Giraffe.

"No, no, Amos," Merlin reassured the aurochs as he pulled nervously at his beard, "I'm sure he's looking forward to your partnership, aren't you, Giraffe?"

Before Giraffe could respond, however, Amos bellowed, "I know why he doesn't want to work with me. It's not because my horns are bigger than his; it's because I'm extinct." And he swung his great head from side to side.

"Not at all, Amos," Giraffe assured him, realizing suddenly his new acquaintance, for all his fearsome size and equipment, was extremely delicate and insecure. "I am extinct myself, at least in my old home of Montana. We're two horned, extinct creatures, you and I. And I'm sure we can work together."

"You're extinct too?" the aurochs asked.

"Yes," Giraffe asserted, "and I became extinct so recently I'm still trying to adjust."

"Doesn't that undermine your spirits and your self-confidence?"

"I'm inclined to feel lonely sometimes," Giraffe admitted, "but then I remember all the friends I have, friends like Merlin and Thomas and King Arthur—and now you, I hope—and that makes me cheerful again."

Giraffe and Amos found, after a brief period of adjustment, they could work very well together. The aurochs would raise a beam on his shoulders and horns, directed by Sammy the raccoon, and when he had it right,

Giraffe, also directed by Sammy, would guide it into its place with his tongue. Then as he and Amos held it steady, the raccoons would join and nail it. They were handier with their tools, Giraffe noticed, than Rudolph and his family back home.

This job went smoothly, as Merlin himself acknowledged, and the windows and doors on one side of the hall were fixed before the Borders beavers, led by their foreman, Casper the beaver, returned.

"We're back," Casper announced grandly one day soon after Giraffe's arrival as he marched up onto the site with his troop, dragging his tail behind him. "And the mahogany," he reported, "is stacked along the river bank in Melrose ready to be hoisted up the hill."

"Fine, Casper" said Merlin, giving his beard a tug, "welcome back. But we have no time to waste. Let's get to that roof. Dragons, are you ready?"

The beavers were somewhat winded after their climb up the side of Eildon North, but it was mid morning, and the dragons, who had been waiting impatiently for some time, were eager to commence.

"Let's hit the slopes," said Persimmon, "that thatch won't weave itself."

The beavers found themselves, after each one had been refreshed with a mug of Borders Mead and assigned his own dragon, raised aloft and weaving hazel and willow twigs into the roof of Arthur's hall.

The dragons, as Giraffe could not help noticing, were as steady and as attentive as Santa's reindeer—and much better at raising and supporting beavers than he himself would have been.

Pineapple, especially, who felt a mother's concern for the beavers, preserved a harmonious atmosphere. "Casper," she cried at their chief, "don't you worry about Co Co: he's doing a fine job. And he's perfectly safe up here on the roof even if he does have too little fat in that tail of his. You tend to your own knitting and weaving.

"Sim," she warned her husband, "you watch those big wings of yours. Keep them furled, Sim, furled.

"He's so awkward outside a kitchen," she muttered to herself.

"Be alert there, Parsnip," she shouted across a gable, "don't you let Co Co lose his balance. And keep that big snout of yours out of his way.

"None of your sneezing now. You know what that would do."

The attaching of the doors and roof proceeded so swiftly that, although Merlin was possessed with the deadline for their work, Samain Eve, at which time his power to transport Arthur's court would be at its strongest, he found little reason to complain.

But he did have a nagging worry, the hall's furniture. One morning when the raccoons had almost finished nailing the doors and windows in place, he came up to Giraffe, who was talking in the shade with Elsie and Amos and Thomas, and asked him to share a confidence. After they stepped away from the others, he said, "I'm worried, Giraffe, I'm afraid we won't have the hall ready for Arthur by Samain."

"It seems to me," Giraffe replied, "we're making excellent progress. The door-and-window crew is nearly finished with its work, and the roofers are over half finished. Look at Pineapple hustle those beavers!"

"Yes, yes, Giraffe," said Merlin, "but what are we going to do about the furniture? We can't ask Arthur to sit on the floor."

"The mahogany is already here," said Giraffe, "and that was your big problem."

"That was one of our problems, Giraffe, one of our problems. For another, I've been unable to rouse the monks and hermits to help with the furniture. They make one turn up Eildon North carrying their bags of tools and, then, before they reach Aneirin, they bless themselves and fall fast asleep—at around the seventh century. They just can't get back here, Giraffe: it's too early for them.

"We've also got a problem with the lumber: how can we transport Arthur's fancy mahogany up here? Amos is strong, but he can't carry all that wood by himself. It's a lot heavier than pine. I had hoped you might help him, Giraffe, but, with that bad leg of yours, you'll hardly be any use at all. And time is passing!"

"It's *our* problem, is it?" Giraffe responded.

"Yes, Giraffe," Merlin admitted, giving his beard a tug. "I thought I could manage everything myself, but I was wrong."

"I'm not a wizard, like you, Merlin, but I do have a couple of ideas."

"Yes, Giraffe, I'm listening."

"I've noticed, as I've been assisting them, the raccoons are very clever carpenters, and I'm sure, with a few suggestions from you and me, they could create furniture fit for a king."

"Yes, Borders racoons are clever and, with guidance, they might make Arthur the Round Table he wants. Good, good, Giraffe.

"But, wait, we still have the problem of transportation. What can you and I do to solve that?" And he snatched his beard right out of his trousers.

"I believe," Giraffe answered, "our raccoons should make the furniture—or, rather, the separate parts of it—down in Melrose. That will considerably reduce the weight we have to move up here."

"True, true, that will make a difference," Merlin said, tucking his beard back in his trousers. "Say no more, Giraffe."

"Besides, if we move the furniture piecemeal, we can avoid any really big, awkward loads."

"True, Giraffe, true. Say no more."

"Once we reduce the loads, moreover, all the workers can help in carrying: the beavers can help and the dragons and even you and I, Merlin."

"True, Giraffe, true. Say no more."

"As the creation of parts proceeds, we can dispatch a few raccoons—each one lugging a chairleg or the door of a cupboard as he climbs the hill—to begin the work of assembly."

"True, true, Giraffe, say no more."

"I'm sure we can find a furniture factory in Melrose and give our carpenters access to power tools—circular saws, electric sanders, spray cans and other modern conveniences—and make the work go faster."

"True, true, Giraffe, say no more."

"That's about all I've got to say on this topic, Merlin, just a few simple ideas. I hope they help."

"Help, Giraffe, help!" gasped Merlin, smoothing down his beard, "you've solved the problem. You are a wizard, Giraffe, a wizard. Arthur will have no more need of my services with you at his side."

The work of creating Arthur's furniture, which Merlin organized as Giraffe had suggested, went smoothly. The raccoons learned to handle electric equipment quickly, although Sammy, who went first on each piece, was not very dextrous, not near as handy as either Sabine or Sigmund. He soon withdrew to the situation of foreman; and under his watchful eye, the work went well.

The raccoons gradually adjusted to the hard mahogany with the help of the power tools. The chair legs Sabine turned on the lathe piled up almost magically. The panels of the Round Table, on which Sigmund and a couple of other young raccoons cooperated, also took shape quickly. Sammy himself, with some help, cobbled together the large components of the royal bed, an act of creativity in which he took more pride, perhaps—that Sammy—than the work warranted.

Soon Merlin started to send the different parts of furniture up the hill. Elements of the Round Table he strapped onto Amos, and the sides of the royal bed, at the insistence of Arthur's Montana druid, he intrusted to Giraffe, balancing one side against the other across his back as Giraffe had balanced bread and mead once back home. The beavers checked in at Melrose as soon as they had finished the roof; and, under Casper's and Pineapple's leadership, they carried legs and panels and doors and headboards, sometimes with two-or-three beavers sharing a load. Before long the raccoons began to pitch in, more and more of them as they wound up the work at the furniture factory. And the path up Eildon North became a busy highway.

Thomas the Rhymer proved a sturdy porter, carrying one whole panel of the Round Table by himself on his first trip to the hall. But on his second trip he paused to share sad stories with Aneirin. Soon he was perched on a stone that was more comfortable, he later told Giraffe, than the seat down below where he had spent five-hundred lonely years, listening happily to Aneirin's lugubrious account of Gododdin's heroic extermination. And all the porters—beavers, dragons, raccoons, Amos, Giraffe, and Merlin—enjoyed a few strains of the bard's long recitation as they made their way up Eildon North to Arthur's new basilica.

The raccoons assembled the furniture in place, as Giraffe had proposed. The Round Table and chairs soon stood in the center of the hall with chests and cupboards lining the walls—all of these pieces made of solid mahogany. The royal bed Sammy constructed—with some direction from Sabine, who also did the fine work—on the high dais at the western end. Queen Isabel had recently acquired a heavy curtain adorned with images of snakes at an exhibition of native American art in Billings; she mailed it to Trimontium by Fast Forward; and when it arrived, Giraffe and Pineapple hung it, in accordance with the queen's orders, to give the royal couple some privacy while they slept. Giraffe wondered about the appropriateness of the curtain's imagery, but it was generally admired—and especially by Merlin.

The assemblage of the furniture, which required some sanding and planing and lots of glue, made a mess, but Co Co and a crew of beavers swept and scrubbed and dusted until the hall was spotlessly clean. "I hate dirt," Co Co confided to Giraffe. "That's why I made the raccoons create and install solid mahogany waste baskets around the walls. I wanted to put one beside every knight's chair—that

Lancelot is so messy, especially in his eating habits; but I suppose that would seem presumptuous."

"Our New Hall is spic-and-span," Giraffe assured the anxious beaver. "It's a credit to you, Co Co, and your crew."

All that was left to do—except for fetching King Arthur, Queen Isabel, and their heroic company—was to install the lights. Since this company would appear at darkest midnight on Samain Eve, lots of light would be needed.

At sunset Giraffe looked around without thinking for Kanga and her ball of wax. But Merlin, now the furniture was in place, had everything in hand—including a supply of oil. He had ordered the smiths and craftsmen at Traprain Law to melt down the crushed silver and bronze accumulated as tribute from Roman governors in past centuries and make, not only a Gundestrup bowl for bananas, but a hundred elegant lamps. "This is the time we celebrate Arthur's return," he had told them, "the time for you to stretch your skill."

Once these beautiful lamps were placed all around Arthur's basilica and filled and lighted, New Hall shone so bright on the slope of Eildon North it could almost be seen in the modern village of Newstead at the base of Trimontium and in the old city of York far away.

But it was silent and empty, empty, that is, except for the dragons bustling in the kitchen and scurrying about the premises to prepare for their lord's appearance; and except for Giraffe, who was waiting, reaching out with his mind and his tongue from the great front door of Arthur's hall to the badlands of Dakota.

Merlin had descended to Boogie Burn at the base of Eildon North to find the seam in the fabric of time that would be the easiest to ravel and then to weave again; Thomas had ascended, not to the Roman signal tower at the crest of the hill, but on up to the ancient ground of ritual fire and renewal at its top. The two wizards hoped, by drawing on the vibrations at each of these pregnant sites and triangulating their own augmented powers, to detach Arthur and his company from the badlands and to fix them again in their proper time and place.

Before they departed, Merlin took Giraffe aside and gave him the bulging black satchel that held all his magic "or all I can bequeath," Merlin said. And he introduced Arthur's new druid to some of his tricks. "I won't be serving Arthur here in New Hall, my friend," he explained. "Once I make this great transfer—if I can achieve it—I must return underground to my relentless love, the constant Nyneve. Then, Giraffe, Arthur's second chance depends on you."

"If you can achieve it?" Giraffe cried. "Are you unsure, Merlin?"

"This trick shouldn't be too hard for me," Merlin assured him, "not near as hard as it was to find the boss a stalk of bananas. I know Boogie Burn pretty well. Besides, this is when and where Arthur truly belongs."

"But what about Isabel?" Giraffe asked anxiously. "She truly belongs in Montana. You brought me over from the badlands, Merlin, and I do not truly belong here any more than she does. Why not Isabel?"

"Yes, I was able to snatch you, my friend," the seer replied, "but you don't belong any place, do you?—or maybe every place—whereas Isabel, as you say, is a Montana girl."

"So Isabel will be a tougher case for you?" Giraffe asked. "She is so settled, so rooted in Montana and, I suppose, the U. S. of A., your powers may be inadequate to detach her from that time and place and draw her along with her beloved king through the seam you will be opening at Boogie Burn?"

"That's true," Merlin admitted, nervously stroking his beard. "I'm not sure I can free Isabel from the land and the connections of her childhood. If not, Arthur may have to cross without her and enjoy all that mahogany furniture alone."

"Love will find the way, Giraffe," said the sentimental Thomas, who had become aware of the conversation between Arthur's new and old druids, "true love will find the way. Those united heart-in-heart no power on earth can ever part."

That eased Giraffe's anxiety somewhat, as he acknowledged gratefully to Thomas; but not altogether.

After Merlin and Thomas synchronized their magical timepieces and departed, each to his separate station, Giraffe stood alone before the great front door of New Hall. He shifted uneasily from one leg to the other, trying with his extended tongue to grasp some sign of Arthur, some trace of Isabel. "It's not as easy," he murmured to himself, "as it was to pluck Percy o'Possum from our Christmas tree or to snatch Roo from the fresh cement at Friendship Hall." Suddenly his life in the middle of Montana welled up in Giraffe's memory: the introduction of Allison; Rudolph's airforce and his assault on the names of the king's subjects; the excursion to Billings; the Christmas gifts for Hal and Ella and the queen; Bo Bo's neatness; Isabella's problems; and the death of the king. "I could do something about those things," he muttered, "and even about Charlton's tooth and Kumquat's hay fever. But all I can do tonight in this strange time and place is wait and hope."

From inside New Hall he heard the great voice of Persimmon announcing the hour. "It is near the stroke of midnight," the dragon intoned, "ten, nine, eight, seven, six, five, four, three, two, one, now!" At that moment when a great bell sounded, all the lamps in New Hall flickered, or so it seemed to Giraffe. He heard something stir in the brief surge of darkness that coiled around him, and hardly knowing it, he took a few steps away from the door.

As the lamps flared, he stopped and twisted himself back on his bad leg with a spasm of painful dizziness.

And then—

"Giraffe," Arthur—it was surely Arthur—"Giraffe," he called from his throne. "Join my dear Isabel and me in a toast to our wonderful New Hall, our wonderful new home. Here," he said with a jovial laugh, "have a banana."

All the lamps suddenly blazed, lighting each step in the approach of Arthur's druid toward his king and queen. Both of them, sitting together at the Round Table in the boisterous society of their knights, were glowing with happiness.

As Giraffe took his place beside them, he noticed Isabel's hand resting on Arthur's arm.

Snakes

"There's a Pictish maiden at the gate, my lord, who sues for an audience." "Let her approach,"

said Arthur. "We didn't reject any one who sued to see us when we held court at Camelot, and we're not going to start denying our presence to any one who sues to see us now that we've come back to the Borders. Let her approach, Peach."

"I'm Nectarine, my lord," said the small dragon who served as Arthur's usher. "Peach is my little sister."

"Very well," the king responded, "please announce this Pictish suitor, Nectarine, and direct Peach to bring Queen Isabel and me our morning mead.

"I don't know, my dear," Arthur said to his wife as the little creature scurried away to do his bidding, "but our dragons don't seem to be as quick as they were in Montana."

"They may be homesick," she replied. "We've been here in New Hall only a few weeks; and dragons are more sensitive, I have discovered, than one might have expected. Besides, Peach and Nectarine are just children; we must give them time to get their wings in the air."

"Very well, my love," said Arthur as he adjusted his real gold torque more comfortably around his neck. "I'll try to be patient. You're the doctor. But where is this suitor, where is this young Pict who's so anxious to see us?

"Giraffe," he cried to his Montana druid, who was entering the hall, "come and stand beside me. There's a Pictish maiden suing for an audience with us, Peach has informed me ("Nectarine, my dear," Isabel murmured), and I may need your advice. Here she comes now."

A lovely girl dressed in white followed Nectarine to

the dais. She was wearing a solid silver brooch at her shoulder, a woven silver girdle garnished with real pearls at her waist and around her head, on which a glittering coil of snakes writhed and hissed, a white silken band.

Before she could speak, Arthur leaned toward his druid and whispered, "Do you notice anything odd about this suitor, Giraffe, anything a bit troubling?"

"Her hair, your highness, or rather, her snakes: that caught my attention."

"Yes," Arthur answered, "that too; but I am actually thinking of something else."

"Her freckles?" Giraffe responded. "She's pretty, but her face is quite freckled."

"This suitor is a Pict, Giraffe," Arthur said impatiently. "All the Picts have freckles. It's her white dress that's strange."

"Oh, yes, my lord," the druid replied. "I have been told that Picts are usually colorful in their attire."

"Colorful?" Arthur muttered with a little snort. "When they dress up they adorn themselves in tartan from head-to-foot, tartan woven from every color of the rainbow; and when they go naked, men and women, or so I understand, they sport tartan tatoos. Of course, being new to the ancient Borders, Giraffe, you couldn't know that."

"I'm learning, my lord," Giraffe whispered. "But she does have a sweet sad face," he continued after looking more closely at the pretty suitor, "and, of course, a fine head of snakes."

"Giraffe, Giraffe," Arthur whispered in reply, "we

49

mustn't be fooled by a pretty face. I could tell you things about my beautiful sister and erstwhile girlfriend, Morgan le Faye—but another time for that.

"Well, young woman," he said aloud, turning toward the fair suitor, "tell us about yourself."

"I am a Pict, my lord," she replied timidly, brushing an odd tear back off her check and a stray snake back under her headband, "a Pict suing for your aid."

"A Pict?" said Arthur. And turning partially toward the Lady Isabel, who was beginning, like Giraffe, to show some sympathy for their suppliant, he mused, "My daddy, Ambrosius Aurelius, always warned me I should beware of Picts bearing gifts."

"But I'm not bearing gifts," murmured the fair freckled maiden, who had overheard everything he said. "I'm suing for aid."

"That's true," said Isabel, "her Pictish head may be full of snakes, but her Pictish hands are altogether empty. Please attend to her suit. Remember, my love, you have brought us back to the Borders to make peace with the Picts.

"You do have a suit, haven't you, my dear? And by the way, what is your name? Or have you already told us?"

"No, my lady. My name is Erip, Princess Erip, daughter of King Nechton Double-Blade, whom, for some reason, you call the freckled."

"A Pictish princess suing for your aid, my lord," Isabel whispered to Arthur, "the daughter of King Nechton: better and better."

"I was named after my beloved grandmother," Erip

explained with a sigh, "Erip, known as the freckled, who died from cosmetic poisoning last year."

"Oh, I'm so sorry," said Isabel. "I'm sure you miss her."

"Erip, Princess Erip," Arthur muttered to himself. "Do you mind, my dear," he said, turning to the pretty suitor, "if we call you Sue, Princess Sue? That would be easier for us."

"Very well, my Lord," she replied with a quivering lip, "although that's not what they call me back home."

"Now then, my dear Sue," said Isabel, who noticed the princess was again close to tears, "how can we help you?"

"My Lady," she responded, giving her snakes a shake, "my sister, whose name is also—Sue, Sue the freckled."

—"Sue the freckled!" exclaimed Giraffe under his breath—

"Yes, Sue the freckled. She is being held captive; and she is in danger of being eaten alive."

"Eaten alive," cried Isabel with a shudder that loosened her sterling silver penanular brooch. "Please tell my lord and me about it."

"One sunny afternoon a few days ago, Freckles—that is, Sue—and I were blowing soap bubbles in the meadow that runs along beside Loch Ness near Craig Phadraig, the castle where daddy holds his northern court, when a great creature with long fangs jumped out of the bushes, snatched the two of us almost before we could cry for help, and, carrying one of us under each of his great hairy fins, made off into the woods."

"Was it the Loch Ness Monster?" asked Giraffe with a gulp.

"No," said Princess Sue with a smile, her first in Arthur's court. "Where did you pick up that funny notion? The Loch Ness Monster!"

"Yes," said Queen Isabel, laughing out loud, "I thought that old myth had bit the dust a hundred years ago—except, of course, in America."

"Then why did the princess say the giant carried her and her sister under his *fin?*"

"That is the Pictish word for arm," Arthur explained to his Montana druid. "I think it's because of their loose scalloped sleeves." And then he joined Sue and Isabel in the laugh at Giraffe's credulity.

For a few moments of hilarity, during which the princess's snakes coiled and hissed with special energy, her problem seemed to be forgotten. But not for long.

"Go on with your story, Sue," Arthur commanded as he wiped his eyes. "A Loch Ness Monster!" he snorted and blew his nose on his fine purple handkerchief. "Go on, Sue."

"It was one of the Attecotti, Giraffe," Princess Sue explained to Arthur's Montana druid.

"The Attecotti," exclaimed Queen Isabel, "oh dear! I've read about them."

"The Attecotti," Arthur explained to Giraffe with a sigh, "are a race of giants living just north of Pictland, who are reputed to draw their nourishment from human flesh, isn't that right, Sue my dear?"

"That's what we Picts have always believed, my lord,

and the giant who kidnapped Freckles and me surely had the fangs for it."

"Fangs?" cried the queen. "My book didn't mention fangs."

"Yes, my lady, fangs that belong on a sabre-tooth tiger."

"Another myth," chortled Arthur.

"Maybe so, my lord," responded Princess Sue, raising her voice a little, "but my giant, Julius—that's what he wants me to call him, Julius—has his own fangs, and they're no myth, I promise you. When he drools—and that's much of the time— his spit drips off the points."

"That must be a terrible sight," gasped Isabel.

"What has this to do with me?" Arthur asked. "No doubt your sister needs to be rescued and you obviously require some disenchantment: you must suffer a lot of annoyance from those plain white togs."

—"Not to speak of those snakes," murmured Giraffe—

"But your father has a band of men as big as mine—if not quite as good; and he has his own druid, the famous Feredach. You are his daughter, after all."

"That's true, my lord, except daddy's band is actually better than yours—he says so himself. But Julius—that's a nice name, don't you agree?—Julius ordered me specifically to produce Merlin and one of your knights. If I fail, he said he might eat my sister and make my enchantment permanent. 'Produce King Arthur's druid and a knight of his Round Table,' Julius said to me, 'or I will choke your twin

53

with my great fin and grind her spine to spice my wine.'
That's his threat, and that's why I have come to you."

"What do you think, Giraffe?" Arthur said softly to
his druid. "Merlin has got himself shut in a stone vault someplace, but I could send you, you and Gawain—if we can
trust him to handle such a quest as this."

"I believe we can save the two Sues, my lord," Giraffe answered with a whisper. "For one thing, the giant is
obviously a poet or a pretend poet, and that is just as good.
I'm sure, my lord, you recognized this as I did—'twin-fin,'
'spine-wine'—it's pretty clear."

"Yes," Arthur murmured, "I got that, I think. But
what of it, Giraffe? He's still a giant, a cannibal besides,
and, not only that, but something of a magician—remember the snakes, Giraffe, and the pale outfit. What does his
being a poet have to do with it?"

"A Poet, my lord, needs an audience, and what will
Julius do for an audience if he eats it? All his pretty rhymes
will go to waste. Moreover, his name, Julius, a Roman name:
that might suggest a certain cultural refinement or at least a
family tradition of something different from kidnapping
and devouring little princesses."

"Well then, Giraffe," Arthur muttered, casting a
glance at Sue, whose snakes were becoming disheveled as
she waited, "what do you suggest?"

"I suggest, my lord, that we quiz Sue a little more
and then go on from there."

"If that sounds like a good idea to you, my love,"
Arthur said aloud to his wife, who had bent over pretty far

to hear her husband's and Giraffe's conversation, "that's what we'll do."

"Yes, my love," Isabel responded; and straightening up on her throne, she turned back to the princess and asked her sweetly, "Could you add anything to your story, my dear, anything that might aid us in solving your problem?"

"Yes, my lady," Princess Sue replied, brushing her hand through her snakes. "Julius admitted to me in confidence once, when the two of us were sharing a nice watermelon he himself had grown, he wanted to be a knight of the Round Table. He told me, while he was spitting out a seed, he had dreamed about it all his life."

"You see, my lord," Giraffe whispered to Arthur, "another strain of human civility."

"He realized, he acknowledged with a sigh," the princess continued with a sigh of her own, "his fangs made this impossible. Their roots do bulge so his cheeks swell out and he looks, poor dear, like he's sucking stones. It makes his pretty eyes almost vanish in slits."

"As if those dripping fangs weren't enough by themselves," said Isabel.

"What about his size, his height?" Arthur asked.

"Actually, my lord," Sue replied, "Julius is very proud of his height. Just after he reached his home and set Freckles and me down, he stretched himself and declaimed, 'Look at me, I'm big as a tree; with my short cloak I cover an oak; at nine feet nine, I'm tall as a pine.' And then he bent down and smiled as if he expected us to admire him. His smile is really kind of sweet."

"My lord," Giraffe interrupted, "once again, note the poetry. And his appeal for approval: that's a very good sign."

"Maybe so," Arthur murmured to his druid in reply, "but I still don't see what to do. We can't invite him to the Round Table, even as a guest. With Agravayne and Palomides gone, we do have a vacant space or two, but I hardly see Julius as a candidate."

"Not in his present state, perhaps," Giraffe conceded in a whisper.

"His present state!" Arthur responded, raising his voice so Sue and Isabel must have heard him. "Why, Giraffe, he would break the back of any horse available in my three kingdoms."

"There are chariots, my lord," Giraffe replied, still whispering. "Two sturdy Shetlands could pull Julius along; and I have another idea or two as well. But let's not put the chariot before the ponies." Then raising his voice, he said, "I'm sure Princess Sue has more to tell us, especially about her enchantment."

"Do you my dear?" asked Isabel. "Can you tell us any more about your white attire or about those restless snakes of yours?"

"Yes, my lady. Julius turned my hair into these snakes—lie quiet, you wretched things—just before we said goodbye. But he promised faithfully to change them back once I returned with Arthur's druid and one of his knights. I dressed them this morning before I came to court," Sue assured the queen, "although you may not believe it.

"I've had such a bad snake day!"

"I can see you have, my child," Isabel said with sympathy. "But what can you tell us about those plain white clothes? Speak up, my dear."

"These aren't really enchanted, my lady. Julius just took my own clothes, despite everything I could do to stop him, and made me don these, 'as more suitable for a suitor at King Arthur's court,' or so he said. Actually, I like them—they are becoming, don't you think?" And she turned toward Isabel with a little spin.

"But, Princess Sue," cried Isabel, "did Julius threaten or abuse you?"

"No, my lady, he was a perfect gentleman."

"A perfect gentleman?" Arthur asked with a skeptical smirk.

"Yes, my lord. Julius turned away as he stripped off my blouse and my smock; he handed these white clothes to me with an averted face; and, as I put them on, he busied himself folding my tartans. He was very neat. Then when I had checked everything and was perfectly satisfied with myself, I allowed him to turn around. He complimented me especially on my red hair—that was just before he transformed it—and said I was the prettiest girl he'd ever seen."

"It would be a pity to eat such a girl," said Arthur with a smile.

"Oh, my lord, Julius would never eat me—or Freckles either."

"How do you know, my dear?" asked Isabel. "He's Attecotti, and we all know—well, all of us but Giraffe—about their appetites."

"Julius explained to me while he was helping me arrange my new coiffure," Sue explained, "he is really a vegetarian."

"An obvious lie," Arthur cried, "to keep you quiet while he dressed those reptiles."

"I believe him, my lord; Julius would never tell me a lie."

"Julius. . . never?" asked Giraffe as he bent down, way down, to look in Sue's pretty face.

"Never, Giraffe. He smiled as he spoke to me and smoothed down my snakes."

"His smile as his lips tightened around those fangs and stretched his lids," said Queen Isabel with a tremor in her voice, "that must have been hideous."

"No, my lady, it seemed quite sweet, as I have said, especially when I felt how careful he was not to pull. And his eyes, when he isn't squinting, are very beautiful, not icy blue like mine, but a deep sensitive brown."

"Sensitive?" murmured Giraffe to himself. "Life," he said, turning toward the fair suppliant, "life is strange, isn't it, Princess Sue? And love comes upon us in mysterious ways."

"I didn't come here, Giraffe," the princess replied, raising her voice, "out of any love for Julius, but to free my sister. Of course," she went on in a different tone, "you will help him, won't you?"

"Yes, my dear," Arthur assured her, and with a glance at Queen Isabel he said, "we'll try to help them both. What do you say, Giraffe?"

"It will be difficult, my lord," the druid answered. "Freeing Princess Erip—as I may call her—should be fairly easy; but, as I turn things over in my mind, I find transforming a giant Attecotti with fangs into a fit candidate for your Round Table—even if he is a vegetarian—that will be difficult."

"I knighted Kumquat, Giraffe, if you will remember, and he crouches at the Round Table nowadays very comfortably."

"But, my lord, that was after Dr. Isabel removed his fire glands."

"Well then," Arthur questioned his druid with a serious frown, "are you saying you can't do it?"

"No, my lord, only that it will be difficult.

"For one thing, Sir Gawain and I will require the assistance of Queen Isabel or, I should say, Dr. Isabel to succeed in this quest. Are you willing to allow her to accompany us into the land of the Attecotti?"

"Oh, my lord," cried Isabel, "of course I must go. I don't quite know what Giraffe has in mind, but I'm sure he has a plan, and I am determined to help him. If he needs a doctor, you know I am the right person. We must save Sue and Sue if we can: that's what the Round Table is all about, helping damsels in distress—especially Pictish damsels with royal connections, isn't that so, my king?"

"Yes, my love," Arthur agreed with a shrug.

"But do you really need my lady, Giraffe? She's delicate and has no sense of the dangers she's facing."

"Arthur, my love," Isabel responded, "you forget I'm

a Montana girl: I often explored the hidden depths of the forest around daddy's palace in summer and in winter, too. Have I ever told you about my encounters with a wolverine and with a mountain lion, much more dangerous animals than anything in Britain including a love-sick giant with funny teeth. Delicate? You almost make me cross, my love."

"I ask you again, Giraffe," said Arthur to his druid, "do you really need Dr. Isabel?"

"Yes, my lord, and she must bring all her equipment, including her anesthesia."

"And tongs, Giraffe? Is this another extraction, one more quest with tongs?"

"Yes, my lord, and a much more complicated quest than Sir Dinadan achieved with so much honor to himself and the Round Table. Dr. Isabel must be in attendance in order for Sir Gawain to succeed in this quest; and, as you have surmised, we will need as big a set of tongs as Vulcan can provide—and, perhaps, one of his medium-sized crowbars."

"Do you plan to de-fang Julius, Giraffe?" asked Princess Sue in a trembling voice. "Won't that hurt him?"

"Yes, my dear," Dr. Isabel responded in the reassuring voice that goes with her profession, "it will hurt as much, I expect, as having a wisdom tooth extracted, especially if the roots are all you have described. But we have many ways to make the pain bearable; and just think of the improvement in Julius's looks this procedure will produce. (I do understand you, Giraffe, don't I?)"

"I can't bear the thought of Julius suffering," the princess sighed. "And what will his friends say?"

"I believe, my dear Sue," answered Giraffe, "Julius wishes, as he confided in you over that watermelon, to become one of Arthur's knights; and that means he must leave the Attecotti far behind."

"Yes, that's true, Giraffe, he must cross Pictland and settle here in the Borders."

"And what about you, my dear," asked Isabel with a dawning understanding. "Will you be happy living far away from home, far away from the privileges of royalty?"

"Wait a minute," Arthur interrupted in a tone of command. "All in good time. I haven't given any guarantee I'll admit this rough giant, with fangs or without, into my fellowship."

"Of course not, my lord," Giraffe acknowledged.

"If I allow my queen to accompany Giraffe and Gawain and you on this quest, Princess Sue, and if you fix that giant's face, and if he frees your sister unmolested, and if you all return safely to Trimontium, then we'll see. That's a lot of ifs.

"And what about your headful of snakes?

"Giraffe!" Arthur exclaimed, turning to his druid, "can't you do something about those venomous critters of Sue's?"

"Actually, my lord," said the princess, speaking in a matter-of-fact tone, "none of them is venomous. Julius assured me of that while he was helping me arrange them."

"Very well," Arthur conceded. "Can't you transform those coiling green tokens Julius no doubt presented to Princess Sue in a moment of fine feeling, Giraffe, my druid, and give her back her own curly red locks?"

"Perhaps, my lord. I have here in my new satchel, if I can find it, a magic comb-and-mirror given me by Merlin a few days before he got himself shut up in a stone vault someplace. Now let me see." Giraffe stuck his head in Merlin's old bag of tricks, and, after much snuffling, he came up with the comb-and-mirror set and tongued it over to Arthur.

"This set," he explained, "was recovered, Merlin told me, from Traprain Law soon after you and your knights had driven off the Picts and recovered Lothian. I have had good luck with it, changing one color of hair to another, although I'm not sure how it will work on snakes."

Then, after giving Arthur time to admire the elegant triskele figure worked onto the back of the mirror, he retrieved it and tongued it over to Princess Sue. "You hold the mirror before your face," he told her, "fixing in your mind the exact hair color you desire; and then you run the comb through your snakes."

"All I want," she said, raising her voice, "is my own bright red. Before he enchanted me, Julius complimented me on my hair—did I tell you that?—and said it was a shame he had to take it from me.

"Bright red," she said, "bright red," as she ran the comb over her head again and again. And the snakes, which had been an iridescent green before, did indeed turn bright red. But they remained snakes, hissing loudly in protest as the princess combed them out.

"Well," said Arthur with a laugh, "I suppose you haven't quite got the hang of that gadget yet, Giraffe."

Even Isabel giggled a little although she was very

distressed at Giraffe's failure and somewhat alarmed at the snakes' increased activity.

"I suppose," said the princess with a sigh, "we'll have to rely on Julius to reverse this spell."

The company Arthur chose to make the quest against Julius the Attecotti had just crossed the Forth below Stirling and was making its way cautiously through the woods of Pictland. The relations between Arthur and Nechton, the king of the Picts, were very strained—as the king had often explained to the members of his court—so, although this little Arthurian band of adventurers was traveling to serve Nechton's daughters, they knew they should, if possible, proceed undetected through his realm.

Nectarine, whom Arthur had appointed as their scout and, when they reached the Attecotti, as his messenger, was flitting and scrambling up ahead through the balmy spring morning. She was followed by Sir Gawain on his massive charger, Oliphant, who had just splashed through the stream and struggled up the bank on the other side. Oliphant was not the most appropriate steed for such a journey, but Arthur was unable to forbid this mount to his knight. "Oliphant, and I," Gawain insisted, "endured the cold together, as I may have told you, on my famous winter quest through Wales to the castle of the Green Knight."

Next came Princess Erip—renamed Sue at

Trimontium—and Dr. Isabel, both wading cautiously over the fresh spring stream on gentle brown palfreys. Isabel rode fairly close beside the princess to whose red snakes she had become somewhat more accustomed. Her medical kit, which Giraffe had stuffed with cotton to keep it from jingling, was proving to be a little awkward. Giraffe had left his own heavy satchel of tricks at home.

He waded through the stream with some difficulty even so and as hunched as he could be. He had suggested to Arthur, when the party of travelers was being organized, he should stay behind. "I'm almost sure to be noticed in Pictland," he explained. "I doubt the Picts have ever seen such a person as me—and I'm so tall."

"Your spots will camouflage you, Giraffe," Arthur had assured him, "and without your big bag of tricks, the walking and the wading should be easy. Besides, I know the queen will need you. I wouldn't allow her to attempt such a quest without your going along."

"Oh, yes," cried Isabel, "I can't do without you, Giraffe."

The princess had agreed. "You're much taller than Julius," she explained, gazing up at him with admiration, "and so impressive."

So here was Giraffe, making his way across the Forth almost up to his belly and feeling very unimpressive.

As he climbed painfully up onto the shore and stamped his hooves to shake off the muddy water, Sir Gawain galloped back. "This is a tough ride for both of us, Giraffe," he said, "but nothing like my ride on Oliphant a few winters ago to the castle of the Green Knight. It was cold, Giraffe, cold; winters in north Wales can be bitter, believe me, and armor is not much protection against the ice and sleet and snow. This warm Scottish breeze will dry us both off in no time." And he galloped back to the front of the little party.

With Nectarine flitting ahead and then flitting back to report, they circled the hills to the east of Stirling, where Nechton's Lord Cinaid had a fort, and then went quietly on, always keeping as much as possible in the woods. They slipped past Dunkeld, the stronghold of the Caledonians, one of the Picts' southern tribes, and then headed due north to a ford on the Tay. Nectarine flew up and down its bank and returned after a time to direct Gawain and the others upstream to a good shallow crossing.

Luckily the spring had been fairly dry, so the horses and Giraffe could wade through easily. But just as things seemed to be going well, Isabel's palfrey slipped and, although she was able to keep her seat by grabbing hold of Sue's snakes, her medical kit was lost. "Nectarine," Giraffe called out, "save the medical kit; the stream is carrying it away."

The little dragon, who had been watching from the woods on the farther bank, leaped up, stretched her wings, and took off. Giraffe was amazed at how quickly she located the kit in the shady stream, swooped down on it, and, holding it in her teeth, returned it. "Thank you, Nectarine," Isabel cried.

"But it's gotten so wet."

"Nectarine," said Giraffe, "your wings have grown big and strong, luckily for us, but what about your breath? Do you have enough heat in that little throat of yours to dry the good doctor's medical equipment?"

"I think I can," responded the plucky little guide. "I think I can." She inhaled and then again and then gave a puff—but with disappointing results: just a ring of smoke with almost no heat and no fire at all.

"Try again, my dear," said Giraffe in an encouraging tone. "Rest a minute until you catch your breath; let your fire glands flex and expand; and then try again."

"Okay, Giraffe," Nectarine replied, and she breathed deeply three-or-four times until she was completely relaxed. Flying down stream through dense pine branches to save Isabel's kit had left her almost breathless.

She took three helpings of the aromatic forest air that surrounded them and then, directing her flaring nostrils carefully at the kit, exhaled. Suddenly a searing flame shot out, almost more than the bystanders could endure; and after another such treatment, the kit with all its contents—as Isabel announced with some anxiety—was perfectly dry. "And none the worse for wear," the doctor sighed with relief.

"I thought I could," cried Nectarine joyfully, "I thought I could."

"It's lucky I removed the cotton before we tried this experiment," Giraffe said to himself.

While these three were attending to the doctor's kit, Sir Gawain was telling Princess Sue, who was rearranging her snakes, about his and Oliphant's quest to the castle of the Green Knight. "Winters in north Wales can be bitter, believe me, Sue, and armor gives very little protection: ice actually formed on my helmet and on my greaves. This crossing was tough, especially on those snakes of yours, but nothing to what I suffered on that quest."

As they reached the bank of Loch Ness just below King Necton's stronghold, Craig Phadraig, a few days later after several river crossings, a lot of rough climbing, and several more recollections of the cold winters in north Wales, they tried to travel more quietly. This was hard to do. Nectarine, who was feeling very grown up and responsible, was careful to fly without flapping her wings and reported back to Giraffe with a smoky whisper, but she was the only successfully quiet member of the party. Oliphant broke through bracken and snapped young trees, and Gawain's armor clanked. Dr. Isabel's medical instruments, now the cotton had been removed from her kit, jingled merrily. And as the party approached Craig Phadraig, Sue, whose snakes hissed continuously, could hardly contain herself. "That's Loch Ness, Giraffe," she cried out, "the home of the famous monster. That's the bank where Freckles and I were playing, and that's where I first met Julius."

"Yes, princess," Giraffe cautioned her, "but we must be quiet if we want to skirt your daddy's castle unnoticed." He himself, however, was not altogether still. He had scratched his shins in a patch of gorse and hit his eye on a tree branch; besides, his arthritic hip bothered him a little; and he couldn't help complaining—not always under his breath, "Why did I have to come on this quest? Gawain and the doctor have the anesthesia and the tongs. What am I good for? Besides, I'm almost sure to be seen. I belong in Montana where I can stretch my legs—and my neck.

"These Scottish woods," he said aloud, "are no place for a giraffe."

Despite this ruckus, however, the little party did pass unnoticed under cover of darkness below King Nechton's castle. Then after skirting Beauly Firth, they turned north again and, as the sun was coming up, headed into the land of the Attecotti.

Giraffe, who had stopped several times to use his tongue on a swarm of pesky bugs that had risen out of the firth and were biting him on the back and the belly, fell far behind.

When he limped up to his companions, he realized they had met somebody, a hermit by the look of him. And while the others were resting, Gawain and the hermit discussed their trip. "You look tired," the hermit said in sympathy. "Your travel must have been arduous."

"Yes, my humble friend," Giraffe heard the knight reply, "but nothing like as arduous as the winter quest I made through north Wales a few years ago to confront the Green Knight. It was cold, believe me, nothing like the nice spring weather we've been enjoying here in Scotland. I faced snow and sleet on that quest; ice formed between the links of my mail. Armor," Gawain assured the hermit, whose ragged tunic he had taken hold of for emphasis, "armor gives very little protection from the cold."

"Good morning, Sir," said Giraffe to the hermit, who was trying to pull his garments away from Gawain's grasp. "I wonder," he asked as he favored his bad leg, "if you could give us some directions: we're new around here."

"Yes," said the hermit as he straightened his clothes, "I've lived here for many years, and I'm happy to direct strangers. I must warn you, however, this is the land of the Attecotti, and it can prove very dangerous."

"Do you live alone?" asked Giraffe.

"Quite alone: I am a hermit after all. But I do have a neighbor, one of the Attecotti, in fact."

"One of the Attecotti?" cried Isabel: "how have you escaped being eaten?"

"Oddly," replied the hermit, "he's a vegetarian."

"A vegetarian?" Sue responded with a deep sigh, "could his name be Julius?"

"That's his name, right enough, Julius Bigfang, as I call him, although he has no use for those fangs of his except to frighten little princesses."

"Little princesses," said Sir Gawain, "I bet he is holding one in captivity even as we speak."

"That's true, Sir Knight," confirmed the hermit. "Do you plan to free her?"

"That's what I'm here for," Sir Gawain proclaimed.

"Oliphant and I will ride against him, won't we, old man?" And he stroked the neck of his charger. "But tell me, hermit, how much of a giant is this Bigfang? And just how sharp are his fangs?"

"He's nine feet nine, as he himself likes to boast, and big in proportion. But he's not near as tall as your friend here."

"And his fangs?" Gawain insisted. "I need to know how sharp his fangs are."

"We must confront him, Gawain, fangs and all," said Giraffe with determination, "and free Erip the freckled if we can. But tell me, hermit," he asked to make sure, "is this Julius's captive freckled?"

"Yes," answered the hermit, "a lot more freckled than that young lady with the snakes."

"Whew," exclaimed Giraffe.

After they had gone a mile along the path the hermit had pointed out to them, all the party except for Giraffe, whose ailing leg still held him back, came to a clearing in the woods. At the far end of it was a great cliff, which was overgrown up a ways and bare at the top. "This reminds me of Wales," Sir Gawain said to Nectarine, who had perched briefly, as she liked to do from time to time, on Oliphant's massive shoulder. "It was below a cliff like this I met the Green Knight—except that cliff was crusted with ice. It was cold, Nectarine," Gawain insisted, "it was cold, believe me."

But before he could put the little dragon's belief to the test, there was a loud rustling of bracken in the cliff's face, and from the partially hidden mouth of a cave, with fangs driping and eyes gleaming most like fire, emerged a giant Attecotti.

"Julius!" cried the princess. "Julius, it's me. I've come back, like I promised."

"But who have you brought with you, pretty Erip? I asked for Merlin and Sir Lancelot or some other famous knight."

Sir Gawain had been startled when Julius first leaped down from his cave, but he recovered somewhat as the princess spoke, and, reining Oliphant so the great horse reared, he said in a fairly courageous voice, "This is I, Sir Gawain of Lothian and knight of the Round Table. I have come at the suit of Princess Sue to save her sister, Erip the freckled, from your evil clutches. Do you have her?"

"Princess Sue?" cried the giant, "Princess Sue?"— looking at his captive's sister.

"That's what King Arthur calls me, Julius, King Arthur and everyone at his court. I like it. Do you?"

"Sue, Sue," said Julius, trying it out. "Yes, Sue, yes, if that's what the knights of the Round Table call you.

"I have kept your sister safe in my cell—Sue," said Julius, ignoring Gawain's challenge, "and you will find her happy and well—Sue, but very glad—Sue, to see you again.

"May I really call you Sue, Erip," Julius asked bashfully, "like the knights of the Round Table?"

"I charge you, Giant," Gawain shouted, interrupting the lovers, "to release Princess Erip the freckled;" and seating his lance nervously, he threatened Julius, "Release her to me or I will wrest her from your evil grasp."

Turning away from Sue reluctantly and glancing down at Gawain in a different frame of mind, Julius said to his armored foe, "I'll open your tin down to your feet, and use your helmet to cook my meat."

"'Your meat,'" cried the princess, "you don't eat meat, Julius, all of us know that."

"But Erip—Sue, I told you that as a secret," Julius complained.

"The hermit told all of us about it," Dr. Isabel explained.

"Well," said Julius, "I can still grind that little knight into my mince meat even if I refuse to eat."

"What a lame verse, Julius," said the princess.

"I'm nine feet nine; his flesh is mine," said Julius querulously just as Giraffe was entering the clearing.

"Julius," the princess responded with reproach, "his flesh has no interest for you."

"I'm nine feet nine," Julius proclaimed, but as he caught sight of Giraffe, who had stopped in front of him and drawn himself to his full height, the giant craned his neck and finished his rhyme with a gulp, "you're tall as a pine.

"Who is this great creature, Sue?" he asked, turning back to the princess; and then, in a stronger voice, "What has happened to your snakes?"

"This is Giraffe, Julius, Arthur's newly appointed druid—now Merlin has been imprisoned in a stone vault someplace. He used a magic comb-and-mirror Merlin gave him to turn my snakes this nice red color. How do you like it?"

"It's pretty, Sue, very pretty," said the giant, "but I think I prefer your hair."

At this point, when Gawain was bracing himself once again to demand the return of Erip the freckled, she herself appeared at the mouth of Julius's cave and, with a little help from Giraffe's tongue, joined the company in the clearing.

"Your sister," Gawain muttered to the princess, "and (turning toward Julius) just in time."

"Freckles, darling," Sue cried out in happy surprise, "you look very well: Julius must have taken good care of you."

"Well," said Erip the freckled, "he fed me lots of fruit and vegetables, but he almost never let me out of the cave; just look at how pale I've grown. And you know, sister, I don't like to be called Freckles."

"I'm sorry, darling," the princess replied, "I forgot I was so happy to see that Julius had been good to you."

"Good," said Erip the freckled with a sniff, "if you call his talking about you all the time good: I've been hearing every day about how pretty you are and how sweet and about your beautiful red hair—red snakes?"

"Julius transformed my hair just before I left for King Arthur's court while you were still asleep. My snakes were black and green at first, but Giraffe turned them this nice red color. Tell me honestly, sister, how do you like them? I know they've become a little disheveled during our trip."

"Disheveled!" cried Erip the freckled, "they're snakes, sister, snakes. How can you hope to appear in daddy's court like that?"

"We were hoping," Dr. Isabel interjected, "Julius would lift his spell, now we've produced Arthur's druid and one of his knights. How about it, Julius? We're waiting, and Sir Gawain is getting impatient."

"Yes, Giant," Sir Gawain demanded in his most heroic voice, "when does the princess get back her own hair?"

"Well, Julius," Giraffe inquired, bending his neck down almost to the giant's level and looking him in the eye, "I believe you made our Sue a promise."

"I know, Giraffe, Sue," Julius said, turning back and forth between them, "I know I promised, but I never thought you'd come back."

"I promised you I'd return, Julius, I promised you.

"Besides, I couldn't abandon my sister."

"But I thought," Julius explained or tried to explain, "Merlin would restore your hair, and Arthur would send Lancelot or Galahad or some other powerful knight to fetch Freckles. There are so many fine, handsome men at Trimontium."

"In other words," Dr. Isabel said, "you can't undo the spell you've cast over Princess Sue."

"I charge you," cried Sir Gawain, whose confidence had been rising, "you will restore the princess's red hair."

"Gawain, Gawain, although I honor your courage," Giraffe said, "this is not the time for heroics. What we need is truth and sense. And this is the truth, Julius," he suggested, bending way down again toward the giant, "you can't undo the spell you've cast on Princess Sue's beautiful hair?"

"You're right, Giraffe. I've hexed my love for ever and ever; she will from snakes be rescued never."

"Well," crowed Freckles, "maybe I'll be Princess Erip now."

"All in good time, Princess Erip," Giraffe insisted. "First we must analyze Julius's spell and find whether it may prove to be reversible: I've never known a spell that wasn't." Looking down at Julius from his full height, Giraffe continued, "Tell us about it, my little friend, tell us all about it."

"It's a spell my mother taught me, Giraffe: she was a famous Attecotti druid. You pour a few drops of this old potion (holding up a small curved flagon) into a glass of orange juice, and any one who drinks the juice will feel her hair gradually turn into snakes. I used real oranges, didn't I, Sue? And I squeezed you a nice glass of juice with my own hands."

"It was very tasty, Julius, although I did wonder why you didn't squeeze any for Freckles."

"I just poured in a drop or two, Giraffe, just a drop or two."

"And then?" Giraffe asked.

"And then I said the rhyme over it my mother taught

me: 'Your head will be a nest for snakes until my fangs are turned to rakes.'"

"A very nice rhyme," Giraffe murmured to Julius. "Now I see where you get your poetic gift."

"But what does it mean, Giraffe?" asked Dr. Isabel.

"Yes," cried Gawain, "and how does it help us break the spell? 'Rakes, rakes,' that doesn't mean anything to me."

"What does it mean, Julius? You'd better tell us."

"I can't," Julius replied, "I just said what my mother told me to say."

"But I can," Giraffe suggested, "at least I think I can."

"How?" asked Dr. Isabel.

"Fangs can't be rakes," explained Giraffe, "but big needles that once were fangs could be: fasten a handle to a long needle or two long needles and you've made a rake— or rakes. What do you say, Julius? Are you willing to restore Princess Sue?"

"Yes, Giraffe. I'll shed my fangs to give her bangs. But can it be done?"

"Julius, Julius," cried Sue, "you mustn't give up your fangs for me. If you can get used to my snakes, we can live here in the woods together. I don't need to be a princess; let Freckles have that job. I'll stay here with you, if you'll let me."

"What a couple you'll be," said Erip the freckled, "your boyfriend with a mouth full of fangs and you with a head full of snakes. You'll be living in the woods right enough!"

"I don't care," Sue responded: "if you don't mind

my snakes, Julius, I won't mind your fangs; and what do we care what anyone else thinks?"

Julius turned and gazed soulfully at Sue with his sensitive brown eyes, but before he could speak, Giraffe bent his head down between them and interrupted.

"Sue, my dear," he said, "aren't you forgetting something? Julius desires to become one of Arthur's knights, and he must give up his fangs to have any chance at that. This is why Dr. Isabel has joined us on our perilous journey. Julius will not be sacrificing his fangs for your sake, my dear, but in pursuit of his own life-long dream. If in the process he can cancel your enchantment, of course, so much the better. But in encouraging him to allow Dr. Isabel to make an extraction—or, I may say, two extractions, you will be supporting him in his own great plans. Love often requires sacrifice, but not always. Isn't that right, Julius?"

"Yes, Giraffe, I've always dreamed about becoming a knight of the Round Table; and if my fangs must be the price, I'll gladly pay the sacrifice."

"But Julius," the princess cried, "what if Giraffe is wrong in his interpretation of your mother's spell, and extracting your fangs fails to transform my snakes? What then? Will I have to live alone in these wild woods forlorn?"

"Let's take one thing at a time," Dr. Isabel suggested. "Even after Sir Gawain and I pull Julius's fangs—assuming we can get them out—he may still fail to gain admittance to the Round Table. Those bulges in his cheeks make him quite hideous, for example, to everyone but you, Sue, my dear."

"The first question, then, is this," Giraffe intoned,

"do you, Julius, and do you, Sue, wish to remove Julius's fangs for as long as you both may live?"

"We do," proclaimed Sue and Julius together.

"Well then," exclaimed Sir Gawain, "let's get on with it; I need work."

There is a smooth recumbent stone lying on the east side of an old stone circle, which Dr. Isabel had noticed that morning a few moments before she and her companions reached Julius's cliff. Placed there magically by the old people, Julius told the doctor, long before the Attecotti had come to Scotland, it was flat on top except for a small groove running east-and-west, which, as the doctor and Giraffe agreed, had been carved to serve as a trough for the first ray of the rising sun.

This stone, which was exactly nine feet nine, "should be perfect," the doctor said, "for my operating table."

Julius climbed onto it willingly. He lay there with his face up as the doctor bustled about, making everything ready for the operation, and then he opened his mouth as wide as he could.

"Just relax," she advised him; "breathe in as I apply this nice damp cloth to your face, and we'll have those fangs of yours out in no time."

It took longer for Julius, counting backwards from twenty feet nine, Giraffe's height, to go to sleep than the doctor had expected—longer, Giraffe thought, than it had taken Charlton. But she had brought along quite enough chloroform, and in a few minutes a soft snore of Julius's assured her it was safe to proceed.

She removed a large pair of tongs from her medical kit and, affixing them with care, rocked first one of Julius's fangs and then the other until she had loosened them enough for Sir Gawain to commence his quest.

He was wearing a smock over his armor, and, at the doctor's insistence, he'd taken off his helmet. "This is not the north of Wales, Dr. Gawain," she said with some severity.

He approached the patient now at Dr. Isabel's command, and, taking from Giraffe's tongue an instrument somewhat smaller than a crowbar, he bent his shoulders to the extraction. Standing near Princess Sue, who had refused to leave Julius's side, he worked the bar down into his patient's gum and, when he had firmly seated it, began to pry. "I'm prying," he reported to Dr. Isabel and put all the strength of his back and arms into it. "I'm prying."

"I see you are," she said.

At first the object of his efforts, Julius's right fang, seemed hardly to budge, but suddenly, as Dr. Gawain bore down, it popped right out and fell on the ground. Giraffe retrieved it and tongued it carefully onto an upright stone. It was fully nine inches long.

Then a strange thing happened: all the snakes on the right side of Princess Sue's head, whose flaming red descendants might make Scotland famous someday (if they were ever discovered), leaped onto the ground and slithered beneath the operating stone. And the same thing happened to the slimy red ringlets on the left side when Dr. Gawain pried out Julius's left fang, leaving Sue for the moment without any hair at all.

"Bald as an egg," cried Erip the freckled from the west side of the circle, "you're bald as an egg, sister."

But the bride's hair soon began to sprout, and, by the time Julius came to and looked up at her, he could say, "Dearest Sue, how beautiful are you with your coiling red hair."

"Yes, Julius," she answered, "I'm your Sue as long as we both may live. And how handsome you've become."

He was indeed a very good-looking, pleasant-faced man. The great bulges in his cheeks, which Queen Isabel found hideous, had become transformed by the achievement of Dr. Gawain's quest into a fine pair of dimples; and when he smiled up at Sue wide-eyed, she saw a very amiable countenance.

Dr. Gawain was also transformed. He removed his surgical smock, handed his dental equipment back to Giraffe, marched across the circle to his faithful mount, put on the helmet that had been hanging from the saddle, and became Sir Gawain again. "This," he said to Nectarine, who was perched on Oliphant's shoulder, a favorite spot, "this has been my greatest quest except, of course, for my midwinter encounter with the Green Knight below that icy cliff in North Wales."

"I bet it was cold there," Nectarine suggested.

"It was, Nectarine, believe me," said Gawain, "the frost, the snow, the sleet."

But before he could once again recall those frightful Welsh conditions, Giraffe addressed the little dragon. "Fly to Trimontium, Nectarine, and report to King Arthur that Sir Gawain has achieved his quest, and that, after a pause at the court of King Nechton Double-Blade to deliver Princess Erip the freckled to her royal father, our company will return as expeditiously as possible to Trimontium."

The rest is history, which tells how the Arthurian party met King Nechton, not at Craig Phadraig, but at the White Catertuns, his southern court, how the king offered Julius Princess Erip the freckled and half his kingdom for returning her unharmed, how Julius refused this generous offer, proclaiming his plan to journey home with Nechton's other daughter, the Lady Sue, how, before he left the White Catertuns with his lady, Sir Gawain, Queen Isabel, and Giraffe, the king knighted him Sir Julius the dimpled, how Sir Julius presented one of his fangs to Sir Gawain and the other to his royal father-in-law—keeping none for his own convenience—and, finally, how the whole Arthurian party returned happily through the Borders to Trimontium, New Hall, and the court of their king.

Picts

"Who can we send, Giraffe?" Arthur asked his druid. "What herald of mine will be able to enter Nechton's northern court? The Picts, especially the northerners, are easily spooked and, when once they've been spooked, quick to draw."

"They're highlanders, my lord, as you have told me, savage and superstitious and violent."

"True. They're Celts, but they're

highland Celts. Who then can we send with a message of peace?

"The Picts and the Borders have been at war for centuries, Giraffe; the grievances have piled up; and neither side can trust the other. The list, the catalogue, of pillage, arson, theft, and enslavement is as thick in Pictland as it is here at Trimontium."

"Surely you understood that, your majesty, before we came back to give you a second chance."

"True again, Giraffe, but the problem of peace looked a lot easier from Montana.

"If you only knew the bitterness that divides us," Arthur explained to his druid, not for the first time. "For years I battled Drust Skull-Splitter and after he had been killed—by me or Lancelot or some other of my knights—I battled Drust's successor, Nechton Double-Blade. With no quarter given. Nechton is as likely to behead a herald of mine as he is to salute him."

"You have one herald in your court, my lord," said Giraffe, "one messenger, the Lady Sue, whom he will surely welcome."

"Yes," said Arthur, "he will greet his own daughter, even if she is married to a knight of mine. I'll send Sir Julius and Lady Sue.

"But what can she say, Giraffe, what message that will heal her father's anger?"

"Not so much anger, my lord, as fear, a fear of his own people or, at least, of the incorrigible northern folk. The southern Picts, with whom I became acquainted last spring when Queen Isabel and I visited Nechton's court in the White Catertuns, are ready for peace—partially, of course, because their fields are vulnerable to our attack; but the northerners, the highland people living along Loch Ness, who are protected by the Cairngorms and other mountains, refuse to surrender raiding and pillage and war. It is the only life they know. They think Nechton's ideas of peace, as he acknowledged these to me in private, are nothing but fear and weakness. 'Nechton the coward,' they call him as he himself admitted."

"King Nechton approves my plans for peace?" Arthur asked.

"Yes, my lord, with certain reservations, but he will split his kingdom in two if he even hints he does, or so he told me—in strictest confidence, of course."

"Then what can we do to foster his desires for peace and help him win over his own people? What message can the Lady Sue deliver to placate those wild highlanders? I don't see any way, Giraffe," Arthur complained, "to make them live in peace."

"I believe there is a way, my lord."

Giraffe found this trek to Craig Phadraig, King Nechton's northern court, which stood just above Loch Ness, almost as wearisome as his journey to the land of the Attecotti last spring.

The marsh outside Stirling was not so soggy, he recognized with relief, and all the streams between Stirling and Loch Ness ran more quietly. Neither he nor Trigger Jr., on whom the Lady Sue was mounted, had trouble at the fords, and the only time Sue lost her balance Julius was there to steady her. "I don't suppose there'll be any need for my tongue in this time and place," Giraffe thought to himself.

But the rocky cliffs and grades—even where there was a path—seemed rougher and steeper than they had in the springtime. Nettles on the dry foliage, moreover, which lined the way, were a constant threat. The thorns of gorse proved to be especially mean once when Giraffe mistook its yellow flowers for broom and plowed through a big gorse thicket. And the white, sticky balls of spit that covered the heather, when the Arthurian party climbed a moor, tangled Giraffe's and Trigger Jr.'s legs at every step.

The little band who made this journey found it difficult to observe the rule Giraffe had once taught Princess Isabel: travelers must be content. "When will we ever get home?" asked Sue aloud more times than once. "How weary are my spirits."

"I care not for my spirits," said Julius, trying to support the weaker vessel with a little joke, "if my legs were not weary." He had walked the whole way from Trimontium, of course, leading his lady's mount, since there was no horse in the Borders, not even Oliphant, who could support him. Still, his legs were not nearly as weary as Giraffe's.

Arthur, who remembered this country well, had urged Giraffe this time to stay in Trimontium. "Sue and

Julius can carry out this first mission," he said to his druid. "I don't want you wearing yourself out and endangering your life—those Cairngorms are steep and treacherous, especially for a lame giraffe. I can't imagine anything useful you can do up at Craig Phadraig. Besides, those wild, superstitious highlanders have never seen anyone like you, Giraffe. Who knows how they will act?"

"I understand your concern, my lord," Giraffe had replied, "and I cherish your regard for me. But I may find some kind of activity around Loch Ness—showing off my furry horns or my long neck or snatching a careless child from the loch with my tongue. Besides, I don't want our young couple to face highland hospitality alone."

So here he was, once again forcing himself to trudge, lame hip and all, through the lonely wilds of Pictland. "I only wish Dr. Oscar had been in Trimontium to attach one of his bandages to this creaky leg of mine," he muttered to himself as he stumbled along mile after weary mile.

But all things come to an end.

"Look," Giraffe shouted ahead to his companions as they descended the last slope of the last mountain and emerged finally from the deep Pictish woods. "That's Loch Ness! Where you first saw Julius, Lady Sue.

"Look how clear the water is, reflecting all the clouds in the sky; and across there is old Castle Urquhart. I can see every stone. What a sunny day, and yet," he continued after raising his head and sniffing the air, "there will be mist creeping across the loch tomorrow morning, yes, there will be a thick gray mist tomorrow. It's perfect, just as Elsie predicted."

"Perfect?" cried the Lady Sue.

"Just as Elsie predicted?" exclaimed Sir Julius.

A few days before Giraffe and his companions set out for Craig Phadraig on this mission, he had paid a visit to Elsie, the mate of Amos the aurochs. Arthur recommended Elsie to him as the best weather man in his domain.

"I used to trust my second druid, Dr. Neil, for weather predictions," Arthur had explained, "but he made a couple of serious errors, one of which very nearly cost me victory in my battle against the Saxons along the River Glen. Remind me, Giraffe, to tell you about that sometime.

"After that," said the king, "I inaugurated a contest to find out the most reliable weather prophet. A warrior, Giraffe, needs to be sure of the conditions in which he will confront the enemy. Several wise men besides Dr. Neil entered the lists: there was Dr. Ed, Dr. Dave, Dr. Marvin, Dr. Mario—doctors all—and there was Elsie, the contented cow."

"It sounds quite interesting, my lord."

"It was, Giraffe, for a while. At first the contestants seemed well matched. And the wise men, each of whom produced strong scientific reasons to support his own daily prophecy, made Elsie, who never explained her predictions, look badly overmatched. 'What an amateur!' exclaimed all the other contestants, each of whom had an imposing set of instruments—doppler radar, virtual imaging, coast-guard data—'what an amateur: she doesn't know atmospheric pressure from adjusted temperature, nor precip in the form of rain from a tornado watch, nor a watch from a warning.' And this was no doubt true. But, for all that, before long Elsie far outdistanced these sages with the accuracy of her forecasts. Dr. Dave rallied in the second month of the contest, but he fell back at last. None of them could compete with Amos's little mate in simply telling me what the next day's and the next week's weather would be."

"I suppose then, your majesty, you would advocate a visit to Elsie."

"Absolutely, Giraffe, if you want a reliable prediction of the weather."

So the next day Giraffe had looked around for Elsie and found her, after a while, chewing the cud in a pleasant glade a few yards below New Hall. "Hello, Elsie," he shouted as he approached her, "I understand you are the best weather man in Arthur's domain, and I need your services."

"Yes," she responded, "I think I've proved myself a better prophet than those scientific doctors—what fakes. How can I be of service?"

"I need to know the weather for the next couple of weeks around Loch Ness, Elsie, if you could stretch your powers so far."

"That is a challenge," she said, giving her cud an especially prolonged chew. "I'll have to consult, not only my ears and my horns to make such an ambitious prediction, but the lumbago in my right hip too. How important is it?"

"Very important, Elsie, the peace of two great realms depends on it."

"I can't quite understand what you're saying, Giraffe, but Amos and I have come to realize how much is at stake whenever you have a plan, and I can tell right now you've got a plan."

"Yes, I do," Giraffe acknowledged, "and it depends on the weather around Loch Ness on the day Julius and Sue and I reach its bank and on the day after that."

"I can predict the weather up there, if I put my lumbago to it; but I can't make the weather. You understand that, don't you?"

"Of course, Elsie. But I wonder if you can predict on what days in the next few weeks I can expect a sunny afternoon followed by a misty morning."

"Let's see: sun in the evening and mist the next day? Let's see. Not this week, Giraffe. Every day this week we'll have good Scottish weather with rain falling straight down. Let's see: next week, next Wodensday and Thorsday: a fine afternoon—yes—followed by a very misty dawn. Will that do, Giraffe?"

"Perfectly, my dear Elsie, and we'll schedule our travel accordingly."

"I'm glad to serve King Arthur with these powers of mine, Giraffe, but Amos, who has a fine sense of social propriety, thinks I should be called 'Dr. Elsie.' What do you think of that?"

"It seems altogether right and fitting, and I will be happy to recommend such a title, such an appointment, to the king. I agree with Amos you deserve it."

"Thank you, Giraffe, I know Amos will be very proud to be married to a doctor.

"But speaking of Amos, I have another topic I'd like to draw to your attention."

"Please tell me about it, my dear."

"Being extinct, although it often depressed Amos's spirits, as Merlin told you, was also a source of pride. It was from that, more than his horns or his massive shoulders or his great strength, he derived his sense of character, his identity. 'I'm the only extinct animal in the Borders,' he used to say to his new acquaintance, 'except for the capercaillie—if you can call that silly bird an animal.' You may remember, Giraffe, that's how he introduced himself to you."

"Yes," said Giraffe, "I do remember, but I thought at the time he might like a companion."

"He did at first," Elsie admitted, "but he's been agonizing ever since you revealed your extinction, and he's become very unhappy, Giraffe, more depressed, in fact, than I ever saw him. Can you do something to help?"

"I'll try, Elsie. And to begin, you may tell Amos I've just received a letter from relatives of mine, not from Montana, but from Africa; and they describe great herds of giraffe comfortably grazing off the tender leaves of trees all over the Serengeti Plain. I'm only extinct in Montana, you can tell Amos, whereas he is extinct the whole world over."

"Oh, Giraffe," Elsie cried, "that will make him feel so much better. It will restore his pride in himself."

"You may also promise him I will talk with him about this topic, person-to-person, when I return from the north."

"Thank you, Giraffe, and I hope you have a successful trip."

"If I do, Dr. Elsie, it will be largely owing to you and to the generous exercise of your powers. I'll think of you next Wodensday afternoon when I stand on the sunny shore of Loch Ness."

"Look how clear the water is," Giraffe said to Sue and Julius as they emerged from the woods onto the south shore of Loch Ness across from Castle Urquhart. "And what a sunny day. I believe I'll go for a swim."

The residents of Craig Phadraig were enjoying themselves in the meadow below Castle Urquhart on the north shore of Loch Ness. While adults relaxed here-and-there, the children looked for pretty pebbles among the rocks that lined the loch or paddled around in the water.

"It's a fine day," King Necton had declared that

morning. "Everyone except my chief druid, Feredach, my personal guard, and the castle cooks should take advantage of this weather and pay a visit to our beautiful loch."

The warriors were spearing straw men up near the edge of the woods, flailing at one another with their swords on the greensward, practicing their war cries down by the shore, or just lounging and talking with friends in the sun; young men and girls were playing a rough game of keep-away with a big leather ball; wives and mothers squatted in groups near the shore, sharing secrets and watching their kids in the water; the bard, Bridei, perched on a sunny stone strumming his harp, eager to perform for anyone who would listen. It was a happy, holiday scene.

Then, while a girl was wading after the ball one of the fellows, young Taloran, the king's mischievous son, had kicked into the water, there emerged from the depths—

A great narrow head with hairy horns, a long pointed tongue, and eyes most like fire; a horned head that rose up on an enormous neck; a sinewy gold neck covered with huge brown spots.

The girl saw it first and fell backward, choking with terror. Then as the great neck stretched over the shore of the loch, Bridei, the bard, who had been bending over his strings, became aware of it, and a woman, checking on her little son, saw a shimmering length of brown and gold reflected in the water.

"It's the monster, it's the monster," screamed the bard, giving his harp a twang. "It's the monster!"

"The monster?" laughed Sir Angus the freckled as

the mysterious head slid back under the water; and leaning on his spear, he gave a great bellow. "The Loch Ness Monster, my musical friend?" he snorted. "Can't you come up with anything better than that old acorn?" The warriors, none of whom had seen anything, were too used to the bard's imagination to be fooled.

"You saw it, Brigid," Bridei cried out. "You saw it, didn't you?" he cried, flinging his harp to the ground in terror, "you saw what I saw."

"I saw a funny gold reflection in the water while I was looking around for little Drust.

"Did you see anything, Kate?" she asked the speechless girl, who was just struggling ashore—without the ball.

"You, you, you folks," said another warrior, Aedan the stammerer. "You would be-be-believe you, you saw one of the A-A-A-Attecotti if the king's bard made a ss—, a ss—, a poem about one." And he joined Sir Angus in a good laugh at the credulity of women and poets.

"But I did," Bridei was beginning to insist aloud, "I did—"

When the monstrous head, glistening in the sunlight, emerged once more from the depths. The glowering creature flexed his tremendous neck and swung it from side to side. His gaping mouth was a black pit from which his tongue thrust out like a banner into the shuddering sky. He stretched in the sun and, after shaking a rainbow from his brow, furled his tongue to scour first one and then the other of his mighty nostrils. His horns twitched with foam, and his gleaming eyes scanned the people below.

That was enough.

The warriors abandoned their weapons; the mothers snatched their children; and the Picts of all shapes and sizes scrambled up the meadow as fast as they could go. The great ball floated slowly away on the loch.

One child, little Drust, was unaware of the monster or of anything except the exhiliration of paddling about in the water. When his mother—it was Brigid—spotted him, she fluttered at the shore in dreadful irresolution. Then when the child, finding himself alone, began to scream, she skittered up and down the bank, wailing in agony, "Dana, Mother Dana, save little Drust, save my baby!"

The monster, when he understood this situation, bent his head down to the frightened child, wrapped his tongue around it, lifted it to shore, and deposited it safely at its mother's feet.

She shrieked, "Danu, Danu," crushed the child to her breast, and scampered after her companions, who had already vanished from sight.

"It was the monster, your majesty, by the sacred antlers of Cerrnunos, it was," cried Sir Angus as the others, torn between terror and fatigue, followed him into the royal presence. "It was the monster," he said, trembling so much his freckles twitched, "it was the monster, wasn't it Bridei? You got the best look at the thing."

"Oh, Oh, Oh, your ma, your ma, your ma, my liege," shouted Aedan before the bard could catch his breath, "it was a terr-terr-terr-terrible beast, terr-terr-terrible!"

The frightened mob of highlanders, crying, whimpering, squealing, coughing, and moaning, had burst in on their king while he was being served his mid-afternoon bowl of mead. As he turned and stared down on them from his throne, which stood on a dais at the great hall's far end, he determined his course of action.

"Silence! Silence!" he commanded, and when the uproar continued, he addressed his druid, Feredach, who was standing beside him, "Quiet this mob, priest."

The druid, a tall man made taller by his pointed green hat, raised his staff three times and brought it down with authority—bang, bang, bang—and, by degrees, the terr-terr-terrified assembly came to order.

" Now Angus," the king commanded him, the first man to enter the hall, "now then, tell us what has frightened warriors like you and Aedan."

After Sir Angus made his report, such as it was, the king addressed his bard, "Did you get the best look at this monster, Bridei, as Angus has said? Quit shaking, man, and speak."

"Yes, sir, yes, your majesty. Even after I saw the monster the first time, Brigid and I and young Kate, I stood my ground and waited for him to reappear. It took just one good look at him to terrify Sir Angus and the rest."

"Where is your beautiful harp, Bridei?" asked the king. "After your second look at the monster, you seem to have forgotten it—just like my warriors forgot their weapons."

"It was lying over there on the far side of my rock, the monster's side, your majesty, otherwise nothing could have made me leave it behind."

"Very well," the king replied with a smile, "you've given me a good notion of your bravery; now give me a notion of the creature who scared everyone else so badly."

"It was the monster, your majesty, as Sir Angus said. His long snakey neck was spotted and gold, and when he threatened us by swinging it about, his tongue, which was long and sharp, whistled through the air like a sword."

"Like a flame, dad," shouted young Taloran, "like a flame; and flaming red snakes slithered out of his nostrils."

"He had hairy horns," cried Sir Angus, still trembling, "hairy horns that coiled and quivered as he turned his evil eyes down on all of us."

"Yes, yes, your ma—your majesty," Aedan agreed, "his horns bristled, yes, they bristled, yes, and his eyes flick-flick-flick, they flashed above us like-like-like the coals, the flick-flick-flick, like the flickering, yes, the flickering coals in Vulcan's forge. It was a terr-terr-terrible sight."

"Well then, my people," said the king leaning forward, "what shall we do? Shall we give up Loch Ness and sneak back into the bracken? What do you advise, Feredach? Should we defy this monstrous invader, who has terrified my northern folk, warriors and women alike, or should we run away?"

"We highlanders are courageous, your majesty, much

more courageous than the soft southern folk you rule from the Catertuns. But no man can oppose the gods of the earth or their demonic servants. This monster will destroy any mere human warrior who stands against him, any warrior no matter how strong or skilled or drunk."

"You would advise me then, Feredach," the king responded, "to flee, to abandon this land which our fathers won and bequeathed to us, this beautiful lake country which has been the home of highland folk from generation to generation?"

The druid raised his staff and spoke again. "There are lands north of our loch in Sutherland and Caithness, your majesty, fertile fields for tillage, green uplands for sheep, and harbors for our fishing fleets and for the long boats of our adventurous warriors. True, we may have to oppose the vile Attecotti to hold those lands, but better to face an army of giants with their fangs at the ready than such a monster as our heroic warriors have confronted today."

"Do you agree, Sir Angus, and you, my son Taloran, with our druid's counsel?"

"Yes, your majesty," Angus cried out, "we can't live here under the threat of that monster in our loch."

"If you had seen him, dad," Taloran shouted, "you would have run away just like us." And the frightened nods all around the hall showed everyone, including the brave Bridei, perfectly agreed.

"I might have run away, my son," the king acknowledged. "The monster, as you have described him to Feredach and me, must be truly terrible. But now, no matter what the peril, I must stand fast. And you, my warriors, must stand fast behind me. I will not let any power, no matter how great or how evil, drive us from our own hearths. Besides, my dear people, once we begin running away, we will have to run forever. No!

"We will stand fast here where we belong."

"But is that wise, your majesty?" asked Feredach. "We may all be killed, killed and eaten."

"True," King Nechton agreed, rising from his throne. " But if we run away, the lives we save will be worth nothing."

That was a good king.

At dawn the next day, a damp misty day, the king stationed his stoutest warriors, his table companions, on the meadow beside Loch Ness where the monster had appeared. He stepped out in front of them and commanded his bard to stand at his shoulder. "Pick up your harp, Bridei, and let the monster know we are here. Summon him to appear before us, and be sure he understands we await him without fear. Twang those strings, Bridei, twang those strings."

That was a good king.

Once, twice, thrice the bard shook the mist with his music. The warriors behind shuffled their feet and scratched at their mail uneasily; the rest of the folk, youths, women, children and all, who had followed their king as far as the edge of the trees, held their breath.

Mist coiled above the invisible loch, muffled its restless play against the shore, gathered about the feet of the king, and swaddled the warriors where they stood.

After a quiet moment of desperate expectancy, Bridei detected the monster's hairy horns emerging from the loch; then he watched its hideous head with its glaring eyes and, gradually craning his own neck, the full stretch of its enormous neck loom in the mist above him.

"The monster, my liege," the bard whispered at the king, "he comes."

"I see him, Bridei," said the king, " and I dare say he sees us."

Turning his head slightly, he commanded his warriors, "Steady, my good companions, steady in your ranks." Then turning back to face the monster, who bent his neck to attend him, he announced, "It is I, King Nechton Double-Blade; who are you?"

As the monster surveyed the force arrayed against him, bent his horny head down toward the king, and unfurled his terrible tongue, Bridei and Angus and Feredach, the druid, who was skulking in the mist behind the warriors, and all Nechton's subjects believed that he was preparing to snatch their brave leader and eat him or dash him on the rocks or drag him down into the unfathomable depths of the loch. And in that moment of dreadful suspense, the bard fainted; the druid shrieked; and the heroic warriors quaked until their mail rattled about them. But the king stood firm.

That was a good king.

Then the monster lowered his inscrutable eyes until they were level with the king's and spoke: "I am Corriebrecken, unmoved mover of the sea. I have come here treading the secret veins of the earth when they seethed with sulphur and when they were baked with frost. I bring a message from Arthur, the Great Bear of the Borders, for Nechton Double-Blade, the brave king of the Picts. I see you are he.

"You may call me Corrie."

"Welcome, Corrie, to this kingdom. My courageous people ('get on your feet, Bridei!' he whispered)—my courageous people and I are honored by your visit. Please deliver your message."

"The Great Bear, my master, whose power spans middle earth from the north to the south, wishes to live in peace with the Picts, his fellow Celts, from now to the end of time, and to join with them, whenever either of us is threatened, against the Saxons, the Northmen, the Geats, the Franks and any other enemy.

"'From this time forth, King Nechton, your foes shall be my foes,' Arthur pledges on the blade of his sword, Excalibur, 'and my foes shall be your foes. Otherwise,' my master swears, 'our two great people, Picts and Britons, will live together in peace.'

"This is my message."

"My people and I," King Nechton replied, "have never courted peace, have we, Sir Angus? Step forward, my man."

"Well, yes, well, no, your majesty," mumbled the well-freckled knight after shuffling an inch or two to the front of his comrades—"we've never, your majesty, that is, we've always—"

"Speak up, man," said Corrie bending his terrible neck and glowering at the trembling warrior. "Your king has given you a command."

"Yes, yes, your Corrieship, I will, I will. What was the question?"

"The king asked you about your courage, and if you don't give him an answer he likes, I'll take my tongue to you."

"We will do whatever the king wishes," answered the brave warrior through chattering teeth, "whatever he commands. He is a good king, and we are his loyal companions."

"I command you then, Sir Angus," said the king of the Picts, "you and all my people of the north to live in peace with our Celtic brothers and henceforth, as my friend, Corrie, has suggested, to join me in friendship with Arthur, the Great Bear of the Borders."

"Very well then," the monster proclaimed, chiefly addressing his eyes and his tongue to Nechton's warriors, "you have heard your king confirm a binding peace between all Celts north and south of the Forth.

"I leave you now to carry the news of this agreement to my master, Arthur. But be assured, if you attempt to break it, if you waver in your obedience to your king and mine—even one jot or tittle—I will return. Do you understand me, Sir Angus? I will return. And next time I will emerge from this beautiful loch, not, as on this visit, in friendship, but in fury.

"Good day, King Nechton, my brave friend. And for now, farewell to you all. Remember me."

Having spoken, the monster withdrew his mighty tongue, plunged his bristling head beneath the surface of the loch, and vanished in its depths.

Later, on the afternoon of the same day, King Nechton ordered Sir Angus and Sir Aedan, whom he had fortified for this duty, to row him through the fog that still shrouded the loch all the way to its southern shore.

"You will wait for me here," he commanded them after they had beached and fastened their boat. "You will wait here until I return."

"Yes, yes sir, yes, your ma ma ma ma, my liege," said the eloquent Sir Aedan, "yes, yes sir," he said, "yes, your ma, your ma."

"Well spoken," said the king. "I will hold you to your words, all of them."

And giving these loyal companions a salute, he turned and vanished into the deep foggy woods.

After hiking a few yards through the trees and the mist, he found his daughter, Sue—as she was known in King Arthur's court—and her husband, Julius, Arthur's new knight. They were crouching comfortably near their campfire preparing to enjoy an omlette made of the capercaillie eggs Sue had gathered while Julius was kindling the fire and had cooked for their lunch. She separated this treat into three portions and invited the king to join Julius and her.

"It's delicious, dad," said Julius. "Your beautiful daughter Sue is a fine cook—an excellent thing in woman."

"Thank you, my dear Erip," said the king, taking his seat on a convenient stone and accepting the bowl Sue handed him. "May I share my flask of uisgebeatha with you and Julius? There's nothing like a wee drop of uisgebeatha to cut the mist. I hope," he said, handing the flask to his son-in-law, "you don't find it too peaty."

"That's good, my lord, very good," said Julius after taking a healthy draught, "and it goes nicely with this omlette, doesn't it, my love?"

Giraffe, meanwhile, had been snatching and eating tender leaves nearby, browsing mostly on birch and maple and oak. "I wonder what my African relatives would think of such food," he said to himself. "And yet," he realized, "I've developed quite a taste for the products of the temperate zone, especially for these maple leaves, they're so sweet and so slick on the tongue." And he swallowed a delectable mouthful.

Then he lowered his fine head and turned toward the king.

"Good day, King Nechton, my brave friend," he said as he approached the three at the campfire. "How are your subjects after their recent ordeal? Has their meeting with Corriebrecken chastened them?"

"Yes," the king replied with a hearty laugh. "Their confrontation with my monstrous friend, Corrie, has left them as peaceful as lambs and as obedient as lap dogs."

"As peaceful as lambs?" said Giraffe, "I hope so."

"Um," said the king, taking another bite of his lunch and a swig from his flask, "these eggs are good."

"Enjoy them while you can, dad," said the Lady Sue, "they come from capercaillies, and, as you know, the capercaillie is extinct, at least in Scotland."

"Don't fret, my lord," said Giraffe, "I'm extinct in Montana, as I must soon explain to Amos the aurochs, and yet giraffes are still grazing and growing in Africa—and laying as many eggs as ever."

"Thank you for that assurance, my mythical friend," replied the king, "but now that I've devoured those delicious eggs, even if they are the last I may ever enjoy, I'm more concerned with things here and now, particularly, with my own uneasy subjects."

"Do you believe, your majesty," asked Julius, "you and Corrie have pacified them?"

"I think so, don't you, Giraffe?"

"Yes, your majesty, at least for the moment. Corrie left them cowed. But once Bridei has turned their fear into a song, it will begin to lose its effect—although Sir Angus may harbor a few traces. I urge you, my lord, to strike while the iron is hot."

"Good advice, and that is why I'll be taking Sue and

Julius for a long visit with me on Craig Phadraig—that is, Giraffe, if you can find your way back to the Borders through the secret veins of the earth by yourself. We need to hammer out a few conditions—now while the iron is hot—that will make the peace you have inaugurated firm and fair."

"I may not be able to navigate the veins of the earth," said Giraffe, "but I know another way home. And the good news I carry will smooth my path."

"Peace, Giraffe?" said Queen Isabel, "what good is a peace based on fear?"

"I suppose, my dear Isabel," Giraffe answered, "we're going to find out."

"But fear, fear and deceit? Can such principles hold people together?"

"Your lord and I would have employed other principles if they had been available. We honor—now as always—the better, more appropriate motives: respect, affection, tolerance, and sense. These are the principles that characterize your king's power and his rule here in the Borders, wouldn't you agree, my dear lady?"

"Yes, Giraffe, my lord is just and generous and merciful. As he should be."

"Unfortunately, such motives won't work, not yet anyway, in the north. And peace, any way it can be achieved, is better than war.

"You remember the struggle against the Survivalists, don't you, Isabel? Your king's motives were good: honor, courage, the defense of his own realm. And yet—well, you remember the result."

"Yes," Isabel agreed with a shudder, "I remember."

"Isabel, my dear," said the king, who had been following the argument closely, "Giraffe and I began where we were and used what we had. The highlanders were hostile and proud and violent. Any request for friendship or respect or mere tolerance they would have seen as weakness. Think of the way they viewed Nechton Double-Blade, their own king, when they detected his mere tendency toward an accommodation with his neighbors: 'Nechton the coward.'"

"That's what we faced, my dear Isabel," said Giraffe, confirming Arthur's explanation.

"Yes," said the king, "but these foes, these neighbors, were also superstitious and credulous, and that's where we started. That, my darling wife, is where we had to start."

"We hope, your majesty," Giraffe assured the queen, "we will be able to establish more substantial and generous principles of peace between the Picts and the Borders as time passes. And, if you will, you can play a part in this development."

"Yes, my love," Arthur said, "Giraffe has carried a request from King Nechton that will allow you to help our peoples move toward a better and more enduring peace. Will you hear it?"

"Gladly, my king. Well, Giraffe, what is King Nechton's request?"

"The Picts, according to their king, have three great needs: latin, cavalry, and medicine. Arthur is prepared to send books and teachers north to address the first of these, and several of his knights, Gawain, Bors, Kay and others, have already been briefed and dispatched to help Nechton address the second. The third, Dr. Isabel, falls to you.

"The Pictish witches have discovered many of nature's secrets and organized a body of medicines, herbs, powders, spells, potions; and they are ready, at their king's command, to share these with you. But he understands you have new and more scientific forms of treatment, pills, surgery, strange fluids, and great machines. He hopes you may be willing to teach these to his witches, whom he has already sent to us at Trimontium."

"Will you teach these doctors, doctor?" the king asked, "and consult with them on your common medical challenges?"

"Of course, my love, medicine knows no boundaries. But I have a question: what, besides Pictish good will, do we get in return?"

"The Picts, who are fine masons," Arthur answered her, "plan to build a broch for us on the Whiteadder Water south of Traprain Law and another north of Galashiels, great stone towers that will assure our defenses against the Germans along the coast and the Selgovae, who lurk in the woods and the moors. Besides, they grow more wheat and oats and barley along the Moray coast than they themselves can eat."

"Yes," Giraffe chimed in, "and I know, my queen, you remember the wonderful raspberries of Strathmore they served you and me at the White Catertuns."

"All this produce," the king explained, "they are willing to trade for our horses, our books, and our sophisticated medical knowledge.

"You see, my dear, we are already putting our peace with the Picts on another foundation besides fear."

"You have introduced peace to all of Alba, my lord," Queen Isabel acknowledged. "I hope it will last."

"Yes, Giraffe and I have inaugurated peace. If he and I can nurture and preserve it throughout the rest of our lives, we will have done all we can do."

"But what about you, Giraffe?" cried Isabel. "Do you want to spend the rest of your life nurturing and preserving Arthur's peace?

"What about Giraffe, my king?" she asked, turning to Arthur. "Isn't it time now for us to think about him? He has helped you take advantage of your second chance—the reason you asked him to travel here, half way around the world from his home. Might he not now want to go back?"

"My dear wife is right, Giraffe. You are more than welcome to remain with us in the Borders. I'm sure I can find something here for you to do. What about taking command of the new Galashiels broch; or serving as my ambassador to the northern Picts; or as the life guard along Loch Ness?

"Isabel will surely miss you if you leave us.

"But if you wish to return to Montana, Giraffe, I'll do everything I can to send you there."

"I have been honored to serve you, King Arthur," Giraffe replied with a painful bow, "and leaving Queen Isabel will be very difficult for me.

"But you and she have one another.

"I am an old giraffe, my lord, and I miss my Montana friends. I have made friends here from whom I will regret to part. But old friends are the dearest. And, if it is possible, I would like to spend the rest of my life with them."

It was possible. What goes around comes around. Merlin was not available, but Feredach, who was sent to Trimontium on purpose, had some of his powers, especially when he opened the black satchel of magical devices Merlin had given to Giraffe. And Thomas the Rhymer was eager to assist. "He's got himself a royal reservation," Thomas chanted, "to reclaim his mossy nest, and he hopes for friendly conversation in the state he loves the best."

On Samain Eve, Feredach gave Giraffe a potion— one of Merlin's powders stirred into uisgebeatha—and, after Giraffe had bid farewell to Arthur and Isabel, he fell into a deep, dreamless sleep. A day or two before he had had his promised talk with Amos; he had shared an afternoon with Julius and Sue; he had given Feredach a message for King Nechton—and another one for Sir Angus. Last of all, he had recommended Dr. Elsie to King Arthur as his replacement in the office of druid. He had thus wound up his business in the Borders. And his sleep was peaceful.

After they were sure Giraffe was at ease, the magicians climbed to their stations: Thomas to the top of Trimontium where the rituals of death and renewal were in full swing; Feredach, following Merlin's example, down to Boogie Burn. And at the moment they had agreed on before hand, each of them focused his full power on Giraffe, on Montana, and on the invisible pathway between them.

"Giraffe's bad hip," said Queen Isabel with a sigh, "shouldn't hurt him on this journey."

"What is that odd scent?" Giraffe asked himself as he awoke.

"It's royal spruce," he said aloud, "with a hint of banana, a trace of dragon's breath, yes, and a faint presentiment of snow.

"I have returned," he gradually realized. "I have been returned by my British friends to the middle of Montana and the comfortable cave in which I made my home."

Is it time for a game?

After reading each story, look at the picture again. Do you see a difference between what the writer wrote and the illustrator drew?

There's at least one difference in each picture. For the answers and other games, go to:

www.GiraffeofMontana.com